The Earl's Misdeed

The Trouble With Brothers: Book Three

Linda Kaye

This book can only be dedicated to my own brother, Bob.

Dear Readers,

The trouble with brothers is that they are singlehandedly the most stubborn, annoying, protective, and yet loving creatures that the Good Lord ever saw fit to create. They insist that there are a separate set of rules for their behavior than for their sisters – especially their younger sisters. And while they mean well, they truly do try our patience at every turn.

Perhaps they were created to prepare us for our roles in later life – a colicky baby, an annoying in-law, a stubborn husband. The endless arguments defending what we feel are our basic rights are often met with a blank look that attempts to insult our intelligence.

Despite the trials and tribulations, a sister must endure with a brother, one thing is certain, after the dust settles, we wouldn't have them any other way.

Linda Kaye

The Earl's Misdeed Copyright © 2018 by Linda Kaye. All Rights Reserved.

All rights reserved. No part of this book may be reproduced in any form or by any electronic or mechanical means including information storage and retrieval systems, without permission in writing from the author. The only exception is by a reviewer, who may quote short excerpts in a review.

Cover phtoo by captblack76

This book is a work of fiction. Names, characters, places, and incidents either are products of the author's imagination or are used fictitiously. Any resemblance to actual persons, living or dead, events, or locales is entirely coincidental.

Linda Kaye
Visit my website at www.lindakayebooks.com

Printed in the United States of America

First Printing: Dec 2018

ISBN- 9781792168635

Contents

Chapter One 1
Chapter Two 9
Chapter Three 21
Chapter Four 30
Chapter Five 42
Chapter Six 50
Chapter Seven 59
Chapter Eight 71
Chapter Nine 80
Chapter Ten 91
Chapter Eleven 104
The Duke's Misgivings 110
Enjoy These Other Books 111
About The Author 112

Chapter One

Lucy Cavanaugh laughed as the dance with the groom ended. Her brother Jack led her to the edge of the dance floor, his smile was broad and true. "Oh, Jack!" she gushed. "I don't think I've ever seen you so happy!"

Jack kissed her cheek. "I'm not sure I have ever been so happy." He turned to look at his bride, Sophie, who was smiling just as brightly at one of their wedding guests.

"Who would have ever thought that Jack Cavanaugh would fall in love?" she teased. Her hand cradled his cheek. "I'm so happy for you. You deserve love, and Sophie truly adores you."

He winked. "I know." Then he leaned closer and whispered, "Don't look now but you're about to be set upon by your horde of admirers."

"Oh, no! I need a break from them." She glanced behind her and noticed a way out. "Can you hold them off for a bit? I'm going to go to the retiring room and catch my breath." Jack nodded and while his sister slithered away he dutifully blocked the path of her suitors. Lucy glanced back in his direction just before she entered the hallway leading to her destination and giggled. Spinning back into the dark hall, she had only taken a few steps when she was grabbed from an open doorway.

A hand closed over her mouth as her body was pulled tightly against the attacker's body. Attacker? She wondered. Who would dare attack her at her brother's wedding? In one swift move, she was lifted into the air and was carried down the hall, away from the celebration and noise.

Lucy recovered from her shock enough to start struggling, but her abductor simply overpowered her attempts. A door was pushed open and she was pushed into a room. "Don't move a muscle," a voice warned. Lucy nodded too afraid to argue. The arm released her body slowly. When Lucy did not move, the hand left her mouth. Lucy let out a sigh thinking this was a lark but then suddenly a strip of cloth replaced the hand that had covered her mouth and was tied behind her head. Another was then placed over her eyes.

Terror took hold of her now and she began to struggle and fight for all she was worth. Her tormentor picked her up and tossed her over his shoulder. As she continued to try to get away, he hissed again, "I said, don't move!" He bounced her a few times to knock the breath out of her, and she went limp. Tears burned her eyes.

A minute later, she felt the chill of the evening air against her skin. Seconds after that she was deposited in a carriage. The man rapped on the top and the conveyance took off quickly. Instinctively her hands went to the blindfold and gag, but they were pulled away. "Don't make me tie your hands, too," he threatened. She folded her trembling hands in her lap.

Over her pounding heart, she heard the man let out a heavy sigh. "You might as well get some sleep. We've got a long ride ahead of us." She could hear him shifting in his seat across trying to get comfortable. She refused to relax trying to recall the voice.

Four hours later, she was struggling to stay awake. Only the cold kept her from sleeping. She rubbed her hands along her arms for warmth. The carriage seemed to slow and she heard the man stir. From the sounds, he must have been sleeping, and she regretted not taking advantage of it. The carriage rolled to a stop and the door opened.

Before Lucy could react, she was once again lifted and carried in the man's arms inside some type of building. She heard the door close and a lock turn. She was set down near a fire, and she turned toward the warmth. The gag was removed, and Lucy licked her parched lips. And then to her surprise, the blindfold was removed as well. Her back was to her kidnapper, but she was too afraid to face him.

"Are you hungry, Lucy?" a familiar voice asked.

Lucy spun around, her face flashing with anger. "Trey Harrow! What on earth are you about?" she demanded. Her breathing came hard and fast as her anger bubbled over. How dare he scare her that way!

"Relax," he countered. "You're no worse for the wear." He shrugged out of his jacket and tossed it on the back of a chair.

She took a step towards him. "My mother is probably going out of her mind with fear right now! I demand you take me home right now!"

Trey smiled calmly at her. "Well, we can't always have that which we desire, my dear." He walked over to a basket sitting on a table and lifted the cloth. "There's food and wine here," he noted breaking off a piece of bread and popping it in his mouth. "No sense letting it go to waste."

Lucy charged past him to the door only to find it locked. She kicked at the door forgetting that she was only wearing thin satin dance slippers. A cry of pain and outrage filled the room. It was followed by her screams of help as she pounded on the door.

"You're wasting your time. We are at least thirty minutes away from the nearest home. Nobody will hear you."

Collapsing against the door, she slid to the floor defeated. "Why are you doing this?" she sobbed.

Trey walked over to Lucy and knelt beside her. He lifted her chin to look at him. "It's just something that needs to be done. But in the meantime, you need to eat. We'll be leaving again in a few hours, and we've still got a long way to go." He helped her stand and led her to the small table and chairs.

Lucy quietly nibbled on the fare set before her as Trey ate in silence, but the food was the last thing on his mind. His thoughts were on something other than the food on the table or the company he was breaking bread with. Lucy studied him. She had known this man most of her life, and she had never seen him this distracted.

She wasn't sure how to handle this situation. She was furious that Trey had scared her so. The one solace was that she couldn't imagine him ever trying to hurt her. She knew he was furious with her brother. And that's when it hit her.

"You're trying to get back at Jack, aren't you?" she asked.

Trey jumped slightly at the sound of her voice. He lifted his head and looked at her as if he had just remembered she was in the room. "His Grace needs to understand how it feels."

Her eyes widened. Her brother, the Duke of Brighton, had mistaken Sophie Harrow for an actress and had spent several days alone with her. By the time her identity was revealed, Sophie was expecting a child, but Jack did not know. He had begged her to marry him and spent weeks trying to convince Sophie that he loved her, which he truly did. When Trey was told the truth, he vowed to never forgive Jack for ruining his sister.

"Why is it so hard for you to understand Jack loves Sophie?" she asked.

Slamming his fist on the table, Trey stood and walked over to the fire. "He is not capable of loving a woman. He uses them, takes his pleasure wherever he can and then he's gone. He'll hurt her as soon as he gets tired of her."

"You can't believe that?"

"I don't want to talk about him anymore tonight. I'm tired and need to get some sleep." He walked to a door at one end of the small cabin and opened it. "Come on, you can sleep in here."

Lucy followed him into the bedroom. He sat a lamp down on the bedside table and turned to leave. "Don't close this door, and don't try to leave tonight."

Lucy looked around the room. The room was small but clean and only contained a bed with one side pushed against the wall and the little table the lamp was sitting on. She wondered who owned the place, and did they know Trey was bringing her here. Trey moved too sure through the cabin, so she knew he had been here before and quite often. She sat down on the edge of the bed and waited for him to leave. When she heard his steps moving away, she bent down and removed her shoes. Letting out a sigh, she stretched out on the bed and tried to think.

She looked around the room and noticed the window on the far end. Glancing towards the door, she wondered how long it would take him to fall asleep. If she could crawl out the window, perhaps she would be able to get back to London. But she didn't even know where she was or what direction she needed to head. She stared at the ceiling and tried to figure out what to do.

There were no sounds coming from the other room. Lucy wasn't sure how much time had passed since Trey left the room, perhaps an hour, perhaps longer. Maybe if she could at least look outside, she could see some landmark that would tell her where they were. Carefully she crept off the bed and cringed when it creaked slightly.

She waited but heard no reaction. Holding her breath, she tiptoed to the window.

Lucy had just pushed the curtain aside when she realized she wasn't alone in the room. She spun around and found Trey standing directly in front of her. "I told you not to try to leave," he hissed. Without another word, he picked her up and carried her back to the bed dropping her unceremoniously on the side against the wall. Before she could respond, he stretched out on the other side. "Try it again, and I'll tie you to the bed."

His words died on his lips as he realized what he had just said. But he wasn't Jack, and his intentions were nowhere near what Jack's had been. He made sure he stayed on top of the covers, while Lucy wrapped herself in the blankets and turned her back to him. He tried to pretend he didn't hear her soft sobs, but he was a fool to pretend he didn't. And for the first time since he hatched this plan, he started to feel guilty.

The next morning Lucy argued when Trey insisted he blindfold her again. "Why!" she demanded. "I already know who you are!"

Trey ignored her pleas and tied the clothe anyway. He didn't say a word when he picked her up and carried her out to a waiting carriage. He climbed in and sat down across from Lucy. She snorted and turned toward the window to ignore him. Trey rapped on the ceiling and they took off.

Lucy pushed her hands down on the seat to shift her position. She felt the seat and noticed it was much more plush and softer than the previous carriage. "How did you change carriages if we are so far away from anything?"

"I planned," he replied. Silence followed.

"When will I be allowed to go home?" she asked. When Trey did not answer, she continued. "I have worn the same formal gown since yesterday morning as well as being forced to sleep in it."

"You chose to sleep in it," he clipped.

Lucy gasped. "And what would you have suggested I wear? I wasn't given time to pack before you so rudely abducted me."

Silence again followed. Lucy sighed her disgust trying to get a response, but Trey didn't bite. She closed her eyes despite the blindfold. Trey Harrow, Earl of Chelmsworth. Lucy had been in love with the man since she was six years old and been accidentally knocked into the lake while Jack and his friends were playing a rough game. Trey had fished her out, wiped the water off her little face, and kissed the tiny bruise on her cheek she had earned in the scuffle. Just as quickly he had carried her inside for her nurse.

From that moment on, Lucy's heart had leapt whenever Trey was visiting Jack. She made up excuses to walk into the room they were in, often being embarrassingly scolded by Jack for intruding into their domain. And then as her body started to change, she would hide when he was around, sneaking a quick peek at him without getting caught. By then Trey didn't even know she existed for all the attention he paid to her. But Lucy kept her crush on him hid in a corner of her heart hoping that one day he would realize that he loved her, too.

And now it appears the first time he remembered she existed it was to use her in a revenge plot against her own brother. She sighed again and heard a book shut.

"What?" he asked.

"You're reading?" she asked in disbelief. "It must be nice to be able to pass the time doing something other than sitting in the dark."

This time it was Trey's turn to sigh. "Shall I read to you?" he asked.

"God, yes!" she begged, ignoring her own outburst. She didn't know how much longer she could stand to sit in this dark silence.

"Very well," Trey said. Suddenly Lucy felt her feet being lifted to the seat across from her followed by a movement against the seat next to her. She realized he had also stretched his legs out placing his feet on the seat beside her. "Might as well get comfortable."

The book turned out to be a collection of treatises on the history of England, and Lucy was quite entertained. She had always loved history and had hoped to one day visit the places she had read about from her father's library. But her travels had been very limited in most of her lifetime. Following the death of her father, Lucy's mother had kept her close to either London or the family seat except for the time she had spent at school.

She could not help but interjecting various thoughts as he read. Sometimes Trey agreed with her, other times he disagreed and the two would have a good-natured debate over their various opinions. Over the next several hours, the two argued and teased and almost forgot the reason they were alone together.

Chapter Two

Lucy was struggling to hide her frustration. Three days alone in a carriage with Trey. Three nights sleeping together in the same bed. She had thought she would be able to convince him fairly quickly that he had made a grave mistake, and if he just turned around and returned her, nobody would hold anything against him. But Trey refused to listen to reason. Her heavy sigh filled the carriage.

"I'm tired of this carriage, too, you know," Trey stated flatly. "We don't have much further."

A most unladylike snort emitted from the lady. Trey blew out a breath and Lucy heard him moving around before she felt his hands untying the hated blindfold. "Our destination is just ahead."

Lucy blinked several times as her eyes adjusted to the light. She glanced across at Trey, but he was looking out the window. She followed his gaze and noticed a small manor house coming into view. She glanced around for any sign of recognition of their whereabouts, but nothing seemed familiar. The home seemed to be surrounded by a wooded lot that grew thicker and denser behind the building.

The carriage came to an abrupt halt and Trey quickly jumped up to open the door, grateful to be free of the confined space. He stepped down and paused to take a deep breath before turning around to offer Lucy his hand. She alighted from the conveyance and glanced around at their location.

"What is this place?" she asked knowing that he wouldn't give her an honest answer.

Trey seemed to study the house as if he were questioning his plan. Lucy felt a twinkle of hope that he had come to his senses. Finally, he turned towards her. "This is where we will be staying." Without another word, he started toward the door.

"How long?" Lucy asked still standing beside the carriage.

"As long as necessary," Trey answered. He reached the door, and it opened as if by magic.

"Welcome, my lord," a butler said as if Trey belonged here.

Lucy searched her mind for all the estates she knew Trey owned. She had been to three, but this place was new to her. She tried to recall Sophie ever mentioning traveling so far from London to a smaller estate. Surely her friend would have cited such a long, horrible journey if she had been here herself. But then again, Sophie would not have been blindfolded for such a trip.

"Come along," Trey called as if she were a lagging child. He held his hand out towards her until she gave in with a huff and marched toward him. When she reached the house, he took her arm and escorted her inside.

Lucy took in the heavily masculine appearance of the home's decor, and quickly assumed Sophie had probably never been to this locale. It didn't seem to be the place a young lady would feel comfortable. As her eyes wandered around, they came back to settle on a small staff gathered before her. "Hello," she said shyly at their curious stares.

"This is Matthew," Trey introduced the man who had opened the door.

"My lady," the butler answered with a polite bow. Lucy nodded.

Mrs. Grouse was a matronly lady who gave Lucy a warm smile of greeting. Tim and Daniel were introduced next and both awkwardly blushed when they bowed. Lucy realized there was no maid for her use, but she had survived so far without one.

"My lady, you must be exhausted. Would you like me to show you to your room or would you like a tour?" Mrs. Grouse asked.

Trey stepped forward. "She would probably enjoy a hot bath."

Lucy's eyes lit up with delight at the thought.

The housekeeper stepped forward and took Lucy's arm. "Then come with me, my lady. Your journey must have been long and tiring. A hot bath and a long nap will have you feeling right as rain."

Lucy allowed herself to be led upstairs to a bedroom. Inside she found the room to be pleasant, although the strong rustic theme remained throughout the home. As she roamed around the room, Tim and Daniel entered with buckets of steaming water and began to fill a large tub placed behind a dressing screen.

She glanced down at her dress and realized that she would have nothing clean to put on after her bath. "Mrs. Grouse? Would there be a robe or something that I could wear while my gown is laundered? My luggage..."

Mrs. Grouse smiled and walked to a wardrobe. "Oh, forgive me. I have already taken the liberty of putting away your clothing. If there is something you can't find, just let me know."

Lucy stared in disbelief at the clothes hanging inside. These were not her clothes. She bit her tongue to keep from informing Mrs. Grouse of this information. She did not yet know what the staff knew of her identity or her situation. So far, they had treated her like a lady and she did not want to give them any fodder to think otherwise. She gave a pleasant smile. "Oh, thank heavens," she replied.

"Well, I'll leave you for now unless you need my assistance," the housekeeper stated.

"I'll be fine. And thank you."

"If you need help dressing, just ring. Tis a shame your maid fell ill, but I am not incapable of assisting you. I've worked as a lady's maid in my younger days."

Lucy again forced a smile to keep from showing any reaction to the story of her maid. Trey had seemed to cover a lot of angles. "Thank you. I'll remember that."

Within ten minutes Lucy was submerged in a steaming bath, letting the hot water melt away her frustrations. She took a deep breath and sank deeper into the water, trying to understand what had happened and where this was headed.

She stayed in the water until the temperature began to turn cold, and she grew uncomfortable. She stepped out of the water and pulled a robe on that Mrs. Grouse had laid out for her. She tied the robe and wandered over in front of the open wardrobe.

She examined the assortment of gowns hanging neatly. Her hand reached out to touch the material and she noted the quality of the clothing. Who was the owner? Was this a place Trey kept a mistress? She shuddered at the thought of wearing his lover's attire, and she quickly snatched her hand back. The sudden movement caused the dresses to rustle and shook loose a piece of tissue paper.

Lucy watched as the paper fluttered to the ground at her feet. A gold inscription in the corner caught her eye, and she bent down to pick it up. "MB" she whispered. Madame Beaufort. It was the seamstress' signature mark on the tissue she used to wrap each item she created. Confusion wrapped her mind, and her hands returned to investigate the garments.

She removed each item, inspecting and examining for any clue as to the owner of these gowns. After thirty minutes, she had looked over each item carefully and determined that these were all brand new clothes. She shook her head, even more, confused than before. Why would all of these new items be in this house?

After returning each item to its place, Lucy found a delicate shift to put on to wear while she rested. But even as she settled down on the bed, Lucy knew it would be impossible to sleep until Trey answered some questions. Growing more and more frustrated by the minute, she decided that she was going to get her answers now.

After selecting one of the gowns to wear, Lucy made her way down the stairs trying to calm her breathing for this encounter. She paused just before she reached the bottom and tried to decide where she might find Trey in this unfamiliar setting. That's when she heard low voices coming down the hall. Lifting her chin, she continued her descent.

She followed the sound, building up her courage and anger with each step. Turning into the doorway, she came to an abrupt halt and gasped. Trey was speaking to Matthew, but Lucy barely noticed the other man.

Trey was standing with his legs spread, hands on his hips. His blonde hair was damp and curling about his face. He wore a pair of buff breeches, skin tight and leaving little to the imagination. But it was his white linen shirt, hanging unbuttoned and open exposing his muscular midsection to Lucy's innocent eyes.

Trey's eyes swung to the doorway at her gasp. He smiled her, pleased to see that the gown fit perfectly. "Lucy," he greeted. "I thought you were resting." When Lucy continued to stare at his bare skin, Trey casually buttoned his shirt as if being caught in this state of dress was perfectly normal.

Lucy shook her head as much to bring her senses back as to answer his question. "I wish to speak to you," she finally managed to say. "Alone," she added with a huff.

Trey nodded. "Alright." He took her arm and led her out of the room. "I see you found your new gowns. Do they meet with your approval?"

She did not answer. She would not answer until they were safely away from the servants. As they entered a small but well-supplied library, she moved away from him and waited until the door closed.

"I want answers, Chelmsworth," she started. "Where are we? How long will you be holding me prisoner here?" She paced around the room waving her hands in anger. They fell to her sides, and she looked down at the dress she was wearing reminding her of the clothes upstairs. "And just whose clothes am I being forced to wear?"

The last was said with such a sharp disgust, it rocked Trey back on his heels. Her question resonated in his mind, and he realized what she must be thinking. "They are all brand new. Made for you. Nobody has ever worn them if that is your concern." He held his breath hoping that she would calm down.

"For me?" Lucy asked in shock. "You had all of it made for me?"

He nodded thinking that this crisis had passed.

A look of pure revulsion covered her face. "What have you done?" She turned away covering her cheeks in her hands.

He cocked his head sideways not quite understanding where this was leading. "I don't understand. I provided you with garments while we are here. I didn't think you would enjoy wearing the same gown day after day."

She spun around and glared at him. "You planned this?" The catch in her voice gave away her pain.

Trey stepped towards her trying to calm her. Other than his sister, he had never stuck around when a lady grew emotional. "Now, Lucy. I was only thinking of your comfort."

And then his words hit her. She inhaled sharply. "How long have you been planning this? Madame Beaufort takes weeks to create the amount of clothing upstairs." Her face paled. "This wasn't a spur of the moment idea. You've put deep thought and plotting into this." Her voice grew louder and more animated as she realized the true horror of her situation.

"Lucy, please..." Trey put a reassuring hand on her arm.

"Don't touch me!" she cried. "You are a vile monster, and I shall never forgive you for this!" She pushed past him and ran out of the room.

Trey frowned as he listened to her feet stamp up the stairs in a rush and then seconds later a slamming door. He cringed. He had not considered Lucy being so upset. He thought he could distract her into feeling as if this were an adventure. He meant no harm to her. This was about making Jack pay for violating Saphronia.

He ran his fingers through his hair, still damp from his bath in the lake. Lucy would probably have herself a good cry and then take a nap. When she rested, she would see reason and know that this was not an affront against her. Just like his sister always did, she would come around and see he only meant what was best. A special treat always seemed to cheer Saphronia. With a smile, he knew just what to do.

"Biscuits, my lord?" Mrs. Grouse asked trying to hide the shock in her voice.

Trey nodded and smiled. "Yes. I think they would cheer Lady Lucinda. Perhaps an assortment?" he asked.

Mrs. Grouse had seen men do stupid things in her life before, so she shouldn't be surprised. But seeing as how the Earl of

Chelmsworth was paying her salary, she would smile and agree to whatever hairbrained idea he had to cheer the young lady. "Certainly, my lord."

Trey's face brightened in success before he turned and left the kitchen.

Matthew snickered from his seat at the kitchen table where he had been eating a piece of pie. Mrs. Grouse threw him a disgusted look. "If you understand how silly that sounded, then heaven help that man," she snorted.

Matthew chuckled now. "This could be quite entertaining, Mary."

The housekeeper couldn't help but share a chuckle. "Friend's little sister, my eye. She's a beautiful lady. I was expecting a small child until all those clothes arrived. Can he really be that blind?"

"I suspect he has something else on his mind," the butler said in a sober tone. The staff had been told that he was keeping his friend's little sister while his friend was enjoying his wedding trip. But when the earl had given instructions that Lady Lucinda was not to leave the house without his escort or permission, they began to wonder what the true story was.

"Well, I have biscuits to bake," the older woman stated and turned back to her work.

Three hours later Lucy was still as angry as when she had confronted Trey. She did not want to see him again today and had refused to go down for supper. She didn't care if she had to stare at these same four walls all night. It was better than facing Trey. He could wallow in his anger towards Jack all he wanted, but she refused to bolster his ego by being in his presence and reminding him of his hateful plan of revenge.

A soft knock sounded, and she turned her head toward the door. "My lady," Mrs. Grouse called quietly. "I've brought you a tray."

Lucy was ready to tell her to go away when her stomach reminded her that she had not eaten all day. She sighed. "Come in," she answered in defeat and pushed herself up on the pillows.

The door opened, and Mrs. Grouse glanced at the lady with complete understanding. "I thought you might want something to eat. There is no sense in punishing yourself over a man's stubbornness." She set the tray down on a table and smiled warmly at Lucy.

Lucy blushed when she realized the staff must have heard her arguing with Trey. She sat down at the table and looked at the fare. "This looks wonderful." Her eyes rested on a small plate of biscuits, and she thought they looked out of place with the fine food before her.

The housekeeper snorted. "In defense of my own culinary skills, I feel I should tell you that Lord Chelmsworth requested the biscuits specifically for you." When Lucy looked confused, she added, "A peace offering, I believe."

"Biscuits?" she asked dumbfounded.

"Yes, my lady. Biscuits," she repeated with a sigh. "If you don't mind my saying so, I believe the earl feels bad for his behavior, but he apparently doesn't quite understand how he should apologize."

Lucy nodded and picked up her silverware. When the housekeeper turned to leave, Lucy glanced up at her. "Mrs. Grouse?" she called.

"Yes?"

"Do you know who I am? Why I am here?" she asked shyly.

The older woman gave her a tight smile. "You are the little sister of my lord's friend, who is away on his wedding trip. Am I wrong?"

Lucy sucked in her bottom lip to keep from adding the whole truth. It wouldn't do to have the servants adding fuel and gossip to her precarious situation. She forced a tight smile and nodded.

"That is true," she answered and turned her attention back to the meal. She heard the door close as Mrs. Grouse exited, and she let out a heavy sigh. What was she going to do?

Trey looked up in anticipation of Lucy joining him for dinner, but his smile faded as he realized it was only Mrs. Grouse. "I expect Lady Lucinda is still dressing," he explained.

"No, she won't be joining you this evening. I've just taken a tray up to her," she returned.

A frown settled on his face. It seemed Lucy was intent on pouting a bit longer than he had anticipated. "Did you make her the biscuits?"

Mrs. Grouse drew herself up at the affront. "I most certainly did, my lord. I baked an assorted of treats for the lady, just as you asked," she clipped with an emphasis on the word lady.

"Of course, you did," he corrected quickly. "I didn't mean that you had not. Was she pleased?"

The housekeeper cocked her head sideways at his ignorance. "Well, she didn't ask me to take them away," she answered flatly. When Trey nodded, she turned to leave but then paused. "My lord?"

"Yes?"

"If you don't mind me speaking my mind," she paused and waited for him to respond. He nodded and waved his hand with a flourish for her to continue. "We had expected a child when you informed us of your guest. And not that we don't mind, as she is a kind and lovely lady. It was just a surprise to us." When Trey just stared at her, she shook her head and left the room.

Trey contemplated her words as he ate. No, Lucy was not a child, but she was behaving like one right now by pouting and remaining in her room. He knew she was angry over this, but she would soon relax and enjoy her country respite. He remembered

Saphronia enjoying her younger days in the country. Riding and taking picnics and walking the grounds of his ancestral seat. But something in the housekeeper's words had struck a nerve.

Trey knocked softly on Lucy's door. He needed to apologize for making her a part of this when she had done nothing to earn his ire. He had failed to take in her feelings in his plan, only considering how Jack would respond. She did not answer his knock. He frowned.

She was angrier than he had imagined. Unless she had fallen asleep. He sighed. It was late, and she more than likely had gone to bed with nothing else to do except hide in this room for most of the day. And then the thought hit him. Nothing except plan an escape! "Damn!" he swore and threw open the door.

Lucy was standing by the window when the door was thrown open. She spun around and glared at him for intruding on her solitude. "If I wanted a visitor, I would have given you leave to enter," she snapped.

But Trey was staring transfixed at the image before him. Lucy was wearing a short nightgown exposing her long shapely legs. The moonlight coming through the window left no doubt as to what was underneath the gown. He felt his body react instantly, and the sensation rocked him back on his heels.

The person before him was a full-grown woman, something he had been trying to ignore since he had stolen her from the wedding. God, she was beautiful, bathed in moonlight and standing as close to naked as possible before him. He was completely at a loss for words.

Lucy was about to lay into him again when she caught sight of his face. He had gone completely pale, but his eyes were burning with something Lucy did not quite understand. It was as if she were a feast and he a starving man. She watched him swallow and his tongue snaked out to wet his lips. "Did you need something?" she asked.

His gaze flew upwards to meet her own. "Oh, I, uh," he stammered and then cleared his throat. "I wanted to see if you were alright," he finally choked out.

"I am fine," she answered with a short tone. "Goodnight, Chelmsworth," she added and turned back toward the window.

Trey let out a low moan as she presented him with a perfectly shaped backside. After an awkward amount of silence as he enjoyed the view she was giving him, he snapped to attention and hurried out of the room.

Once safely away from her tempting display, he covered his face with both hands and tried to rub the impure thoughts away. "Holy hell," he whispered to himself.

The door closed, and Lucy turned back to make certain he was gone. Midway through her turn, she caught her reflection in the mirror and gasped in horror when she realized the moonlight had made the material completely see-through! No wonder Trey had been staring at her so strange and behaved so odd.

Her hands covered her body as if to protect herself from his gaze. From his heated gaze. Slowly the knowledge registered in her mind. He had been shocked, but he had not turned away. The sight of her had put him off balance, had shaken him, weakened him. A smile formed on her lips. Perhaps she could keep him off guard, distract him from his goal of revenge on Jack. And when he was at his weakest, she would use that to convince him to give up.

Feeling much better than she had in days, she climbed into bed, resolved that starting tomorrow morning, she would be on a new path. She would convince Trey of his error and in doing so, save herself from ruination and her brother from a lifetime of hate and anger toward his oldest and closest friend.

Chapter Three

Trey jumped to his feet in surprise when Lucy entered the dining room the following morning. He wasn't sure if she would make an appearance today or if she would remain holed up in her room. He gave her a warm smile as he took in how lovely Lucy looked in her pink day dress. "Good morning," he greeted.

Lucy raised her chin slightly before answering. "Good morning," she returned and approached the table.

The earl moved quickly to help her into her chair. He froze when her light floral perfume danced under his nose. An image of Lucy in that sheer nightgown flashed in his mind, and he shook his head to regain his senses.

"I'm glad you decided to join me this morning," he noted as he resumed his seat.

Lucy took a deep breath. She could do this. She would be pleasant and charming, but she also knew that she could not be too obvious in her change in mood. "I was hungry and tired of looking at the same walls," she answered quietly.

Trey swallowed. "Lucy, I wanted to apologize for bringing you into this. I have no anger toward you, and I failed to take your feelings into consideration." He waited for her to meet his gaze, but she did not.

"But you still won't let me go home?" she asked even as she knew the answer before the words left her mouth.

He sighed. "I'm sorry, but not yet." He felt a twinge of guilt at her crestfallen expression. "But perhaps you can look at this as a respite and enjoy the beautiful countryside." He gave her a hopeful smile.

Lucy raised her head and pinned him with one of her mother's famous exasperated stares. "And what am I to do for entertainment? Are you planning on hosting a ball or holding a musical or perhaps there is a theater set up in the stable? A museum in the attic?"

"There might very well be a museum up there. I haven't had a chance to explore the entire property." He chuckled trying to lighten the mood.

Seizing the opportunity to feign forgiveness. She stared at him for a few seconds before giving over to a grin. "Perhaps we can investigate it while we are here."

Trey let out a sigh of relief, hoping her anger had passed. "That sounds like a fine idea." He nodded to Tim, the footman, to begin serving but the young man was in the middle of trying to discreetly yawn. Trey had to clear his throat twice to get the man's attention.

Tim blushed at being caught, but Lucy smiled. She could only imagine what the young man had been doing last night to cause him to lose sleep. When he sat her plate of food down, she looked at him and asked, "Did somebody have a late night, Tim?" Her smile increased as his entire neck and face turned to a brilliant red.

"I'm sorry, my lady. It won't happen again," he muttered.

She waved him off with a chuckle. "I am well accustomed to my own brother's late hours. Please don't apologize to me."

Trey's face had paled during the back and forth between the two. After the sight of Lucy in her sheer nightgown, he could not possibly sleep in the same bed as her. Nor could he allow her the chance to escape in the night. And so he had enlisted Tim and Daniel to guard the door to her room and the balcony all night. Even as he laid in his own bed in the connecting room, he could not sleep, the sight of her perfectly shaped form running through his mind.

"Tim, if you need to catch up on your sleep, I image we can fend for ourselves for a few hours," he said in a bored tone. "Daniel, as well, if he is as tired as you."

Tim nodded thankfully and fled the room.

Lucy giggled. "I suspect those two will be tucked in their own beds early tonight. At least that's Jack's usual habit." At the mention of her brother's name, Trey's smile faded quickly. Lucy frowned and turned her attention to her food.

The couple ate in silence until Trey knew he had to break the tension that had grown. "What are your plans for today?" Immediately he regretted the words.

She pinned him with an annoyed stare. "What are my options?" she asked flatly.

"Well, what is it that you ladies normally do every day?" he tried.

She rolled her eyes. "Well, we make calls, take tea, attend musicals, visit modistes, oh, and of course we rest for the upcoming evening social events." She sighed in an exaggerated manner. "Alas, none of that seems possible here."

He let out an audible sign. "Look, I understand you are not pleased, but while we are here can you at least put forth an effort to try to enjoy yourself?"

She threw her linen napkin on the plate and cocked her head at him. "Will you give me a tour of the place then or shall I ask Mrs. Grouse?"

"I'd be happy to," he said relieved that she was being agreeable. "But I must warn you, I'm not all that familiar with the place myself." He stood and walked to assist her from her chair.

Lucy took his hand as she rose and raised an eyebrow. "Perhaps Mrs. Grouse should give us both the tour then?" She carefully leaned closer to him and gave him a smile. "Or it could be an adventure to figure it all out ourselves."

He found himself smiling back at her, drawn into her invitation. He didn't want to share her with anybody. A shiver ran down his spine reminding him of who this beautiful lady was. He took a half step away casually trying not to show his discomfort at being so near to her. "Shall we?" She nodded and placed her hand on his arm feeling him tense at her touch. Inwardly she grinned, knowing that he was already struggling.

They ascended the stairs together after exploring the rooms on the lower level and finding it perfectly serviceable. Lucy felt more comfortable on the second floor. The landing opening into a large open hall with doors leading to the dining room, a sitting room, and a library that appeared to double as a study. Lucy immediately went to scan the shelves of the library.

"Is there anything good there?" he asked as he approached and stood behind her.

Lucy felt his presence and shifted her shoulders back slightly, so her skirts would just lightly brush against his legs. She heard his sharp intake of breath at the sensation and congratulated herself for once again making him uncomfortable.

"It appears to be a standard library filled with the basics. Have you not explored it before?"

"No, the few times I have been here I had other pursuits on my mind," he answered.

She turned to face him and found herself a mere two inches from his body. "Oh? And what pursuits are more intriguing?" she asked innocently.

His eyes drifted to her upturned face. Her lips were plump and pink and begging to be kissed. A single curl had worked its way from her coiffure and laid against her porcelain cheek. His hand raised of its own accord to brush the strands back behind her ear. Damn, how had he not noticed what a stunning lady Lucy had grown to be? Had he just always looked at her as his little sister's friend and never saw the truth as it stood before him now?

"Well?" she asked softly.

Trey was snapped back from his thoughts. "Well what?" he repeated dumbfounded.

She chuckled. "What pursuits do you find more intriguing than a good library?"

He shook his head. "Oh. Well, I enjoy fishing."

"Fishing?"

He took a breath a stepped back from this temptation. "Yes. Fishing. Father used to take me fishing as a lad, and I still find it relaxing."

"And what did Sophie do to pass the time while she was here?"

His brow furrowed in confusion. "Sophie? She's never been here. I've just recently purchased the place."

"Oh," she replied. She tilted her head to one side. "Why would you purchase a place so far from London?"

He grinned at her. "The fishing is good."

Lucy stared at him in disbelief briefly before she began to giggle. "I don't think I will ever understand men!" She let her hand rest ever so lightly and casually on his chest for the slightest moment before she turned back to the shelves. "Well, your reading selection is tolerable but could definitely use some additions."

"Perhaps you can make me a list of what my needs are?" He coughed to cover the slight moan from his misspoken double entendre.

Lucy spun toward him at his words. His eyes seemed to burn into hers, and she innocently licked her lips in order to form words. "I would be more than happy to help you with what you need," she whispered so softly he thought he must have misheard her.

Trey's body instantly reacted to her unintended offer. He swallowed hard. Twice. Taking a deep breath, he gave her a forced smile. "I would appreciate that."

"Shall we continue to the bedchambers?" she asked innocently.

"What?" he asked in shock. He had to have heard her wrong.

Lucy's pride swelled at how pale his face turned. She knew that she was pushing him to his limits, but that was precisely where she wanted him. Off balanced and unsure. "Our tour," she reminded gently.

"Oh," he answered and nodded.

Once upstairs, Trey made sure to keep a considerable distance from this little vixen. If only she knew what she was doing to him! He refused to even consider that she was aware of how she was affecting him.

"Five rooms. Very charming," she commented as Trey closed the last door. "It's much larger than it appears from the outside." The bedrooms were small but comfortable. She glanced at the narrow stairs leading to the upper level. "Are the servants' rooms up there?"

Trey shrugged. "None that are being used. Tim and Daniel prefer the room in the stable, and Matthew and Mrs. Grouse share a room on the ground floor near the kitchen."

Lucy gasped and looked wide-eyed at him. "You aren't serious?"

He grinned. "They are married, after all."

Slowly a giggle escaped her. "Then I suppose that is acceptable. My heavens for a moment I was..." Her words faded as she realized how naive she nearly sounded combined with the fact that Trey had slept in her bed every night except the previous night.

Trey fought the blush that threatened to cover his face. "Perhaps we can save the upper floor for later. I'm starving, and I believe I smell luncheon."

Lucy nodded. "That sounds fine." Trey didn't offer to take her arm as he headed for the lower level. Lucy stared at his broad back as he descended the stairs in front of her.

That night as Lucy paced in her bedchamber she couldn't help but feel as if her plan had taken a step backward. Trey had been quiet since their tour, barely saying a word during their luncheon and then disappearing into the study for the rest of the day. Following supper, he had returned to his study and closed the door. She sighed.

She could have wiled away the time reading, but by closing the study door, Trey had made it clear he did not want to be disturbed by her. She was left to roam aimlessly, visiting with Mrs. Grouse in the kitchen and even helping her peel potatoes.

And now she wasn't the least bit tired. She would love to select a book from the library and read in bed, but Trey had given no indication of leaving his domain. She flopped down into a chair, preparing to undress for the evening when she heard a noise in the room beside her own.

Trey! She had wondered where he was sleeping. With him already in his bedchamber perhaps she could sneak down to find a book tonight in case he shut himself up in the room tomorrow. She bit her lip as she listened to his movements, waiting for him to settle down. When several minutes had passed without a sound, she tiptoed towards the door.

She prayed the door would not make a sound as she carefully turned the handle and pulled it toward her. She stuck her head out and glanced both ways down the hall. She did not see anybody, so she took a step out of the room until she could see his door. It was closed. She smiled, letting out a breath that he would not hear her before she took another step.

"Going somewhere?" a voice asked from behind her.

Lucy screamed and spun around to find Trey standing in her bedroom. "Trey! How did you get in here?" He had removed his jacket and cravat. His shirt was unbuttoned at the top revealing a patch of golden curls on his chest.

"You answer my question first," he growled.

"A book!" she snapped. "I was going to get a book to help me sleep."

"A book, eh?" he mocked. He snorted and shook his head. She was going to sneak out. "You expect me to believe that?" He walked towards her in an ominous manner until he took her arm and pulled her back into the room. He shut the door with a bang.

He turned to face her, and she stepped backward. He continued to stalk her until she was pressed against the wall. Trey's hand lifted her chin until she was forced to look in his eyes. "Lucy, you have no idea where you are. You don't know who or even where to find help. There could be brigands and beasts that would love to find you stumbling about in the dark."

Lucy trembled at his touch. She swallowed. She refused to let him scare her. "You are correct, my lord. One never knows when they will be stolen away and held prisoner," she challenged.

Rather than appear chastised, Trey merely smirked. He leaned closer until his breath was caressing her cheek. "Then I suggest you get yourself in bed before your current jailer decides to teach you a lesson you won't soon forget."

Lucy caught the slightest hint of brandy on his breath and knew that he would not listen to anything she said now. She huffed her frustration and stomped away from him. She grabbed her nightgown from the back of a chair and turned on him. "If you don't mind, would you please leave while I dress?"

Trey chuckled. "No," he clipped and pointed toward the dressing screen. Without another word, he moved to the bed and leaned across it, placing pillows down the middle. When he stretched out on top of the covers, Lucy shrieked her anger and stamped off behind the screen.

After much unladylike murmurs and slurs, Lucy reappeared wearing a blue lace gown that accentuated her curves and contours. Trey blinked and inwardly cursed himself for not stressing to the dressmaker he wanted modest night clothes. Lucy glared at him, but walked straight to the bed and climbed in, covering herself from his stunned gaze.

"Are you happy?" she hissed.

"I am tired," he answered and rolled onto his side putting his back to her. His manhood had sprung to life and he didn't know how he would survive with her in the same bed and so desirable. The alcohol fog lifted for a second, and he scolded himself for thinking Lucy desirable. He closed his eyes, but his last thought was how much he wanted to throw these pillows aside and show her just how he was feeling.

Chapter Four

The next morning over breakfast Trey asked Lucy what her plans were for the day. She paused in mid-bite, her fork left hanging in the air. Slowly she lowered her hand and set the utensil down. "Well, that depends on if I will be allowed in the library to select a book to occupy my long tedious hours inside your private prison."

Trey frowned. "You could have knocked."

"Or I could be back in my own home, not worrying about where my boundaries are or wondering what fresh air is like or if my mother is worried to death over me," she countered.

"Can't you try to cooperate with me? I am trying to make this as comfortable as possible for you?" he reasoned. Although he hadn't factored in how uncomfortable this ordeal would turn out for him as a vision of her in that sheer gown filled his mind.

Lucy signed. "Very well. What are your plans for the day?"

"I was going to go fishing," he answered. "Care to join me?"

"Fishing?" she asked in disbelief. She was a woman, not a child. But perhaps spending more time in his presence would chip away his defenses. "I haven't been fishing since I was a child, but I shall do my best to enjoy it."

Trey smiled. "I'll ask Mrs. Grouse to pack us a luncheon. It will do us both good to enjoy the fresh air." And perhaps he wouldn't feel as if her nearness caused the walls to close in on him. He motioned to Daniel.

Lucy couldn't hear what was said, but the footman nodded and hurried from the room. "Bringing in co-conspirators now?" she teased.

He took a bite and raised his eyebrows until he could swallow. "Well, unless you are volunteering to go dig for worms."

She scrunched up her face and shook her head. "Daniel has my sympathies," she answered.

He chuckled and resumed his meal.

"You truly enjoy fishing?" she asked as they walked arm in arm toward the lake.

Trey smiled down at her warmly. "I seem to recall you once enjoyed the sport. Or at least you always wanted to tag along with Jack and myself." His smile quickly slipped away at the mention of the man who had seduced his sister.

Lucy noticed his changed expression but wanted to keep the mood light. "Perhaps I just enjoyed the company. It could be awfully lonely for a little girl out in the country. The boys could run wild and have a jolly good time whereas a girl was expected first and foremost to stay clean and act ladylike. It didn't seem fair."

"You sound like Saphronia," he replied. "She would get so angry when mother made her practice the pianoforte while I went riding and hunting."

She giggled. "I remember your mother telling Sophie and myself the importance of learning to play. She said it would be relaxing and soothing for our future husbands after a long day. But I also remember your father blushing when I caught him rolling his eyes at her reasoning."

Trey smiled and then suddenly stopped walking as her words registered. "Do you remember my parents, then?" She nodded. "Saphronia rarely speaks of them, and I sometimes wondered if she was too young to remember them."

Lucy faced him. He looked so lost. She reached one hand up to cradle his cheek and the other rested against his chest. "Oh, Trey," she whispered. "She remembers them. She remembers their love and the laughter in your home. And she remembers when they left." She gave him an encouraging smile.

Trey had been touched by more women than he could count over his lifetime. Mostly for seduction, sometimes for favors, and often for his attention. But he couldn't ever recall a woman touching him for comfort, as Lucy was doing now. His head leaned into her touch, and he closed his eyes for the briefest of moments.

Lucy realized in that instant, there was a lot more to Trey than she had ever considered. He wasn't just a protective brother. He was Sophie's only protection, and he had been fighting to protect her future as well as her past. "You know, she used to make the rest of us so jealous of her big brother."

Trey was shaken from his trance by her words. "Jealous? How?"

She giggled. "Well, my brother never had tea parties with me. And my brother certainly never read me a bedtime story. And when I was sick, my brother never considered sitting by my bedside all night long. And he never once took the time while I paraded dress after dress before him to help me select the perfect one to wear to my first tea."

The earl laughed. "She's told on me?"

"No, she *bragged* on you!"

He laughed again. "I shall have to discuss with her about keeping my secrets."

"I thought it was very sweet of you to treat her so well," Lucy stated.

Wanting to change the subject before he was too embarrassed to look at her again, Trey held his arm out to her. "Shall we?" Lucy took his arm, and they continued their way to the lake.

After placing a blanket on the ground, Trey helped her sit and then positioned two poles and a small bucket of dirt between them. He handed one pole to Lucy and proceeded to dig around in the pail of dirt. After finding a worm, he baited his hook and then noticed Lucy watching him. "Aren't you going to bait your hook?" he asked.

She wrinkled her nose and gingerly reached towards the dirt. She grabbed a worm laying on top, but the second she picked it up, it began to move. She screamed and shook her hand, sending the worm flying into the lake. Trey laughed at her and she glared at him.

"What's wrong?" he chuckled.

"It was icky!" she shrieked.

"Icky?" his mirth growing. "Is that a real word?"

She wiped her hand on the ground, her face still wrinkled in disgust. "It is today."

Laughing, he handed her the pole that he had already baited. "Here, darling. I wouldn't want you to get icky."

Lucy triumphantly took the pole. "Thank you, my lord," she cooed.

After he finished baiting his hook, he cast both her line and his and then leaned back. They sat in silence for quite a while, just taking in the peacefulness of the setting. It was beautiful. The lake sat down in a small valley with a thick forest behind them and a rolling hill before them. It was as if they had been dropped into their own secluded hideout.

She broke the silence. "It is so beautiful here. I can see how you could relax and clear your mind here." When Trey didn't respond, she turned towards him. "I think you need a boat."

"A boat?" he asked.

She shrugged. "I think a boat would be relaxing. Isn't that why you fish? To relax?"

Trey looked at her. She looked so adorable today and was being such a good sport despite not wanting to touch a worm. "It's part of it," he answered. "My father used to take me fishing quite a bit. It was our special time. He wasn't Chelmsworth or an aristocrat. He was just a father spending time with his son. I miss those times."

Lucy realized a sadness had settled over him, and she couldn't help but feel his pain. "I was the same age as you when my father died. But I was fortunate enough to have my mother there." Her heart clenched at the memory of when her father died so unexpectantly. "How did you do it?" she asked.

"Not well at all," he replied thinking of how he had broken down and cried for days, avoiding everybody including his sister. The pressure of his new responsibilities had consumed him until he ran away from it all, thinking if he hid long enough everything would go back to the way it was.

Her head snapped up at his answer. It was not what she had expected him to say. "What do you mean? Everybody talks about how well you stepped up to the responsibilities of your title and your sister."

He sighed. "I ran away," he admitted. "Not one of my prouder moments, but I fled as soon as the funeral was over. I left my sister, I left my responsibilities, I left it all," he admitted.

Lucy reached over and took his hand. "But you came back, and that makes you one of the bravest men I know." When he didn't respond, she added, "Jack ran off when Father died."

He snorted. Jack had gone on a three-day drunk, dragging most of their set with him. But he had never run. He was still in London, just not at home with his family.

"Well, he did," she insisted. "I heard the servants talking about how Mother tracked him down to a club and made him leave."

Trey couldn't hide his mirth at her naive description of it. A more honest description would be that the Dowager Duchess of Brighton had stormed their gentleman's club, grabbed her son by the ear, publicly berated him, and then turned her wrath on the rest of them. Not a single man had dared lift a finger to defend Jack, and the new Duke of Brighton was pulled out of there by his mother while she scolded and at one time actually spanked his behind.

"What's so funny?" she demanded.

"I was there when that happened." He could laugh about it now, but it was one of the most terrifying sights he had ever dealt with at the time.

Lucy's eyes widened. "Did she scold him good?"

He chuckled. "I was running for my life by the time she finished with him. Your mother is quite a formidable lady."

Before Lucy could respond she heard a small splash from the lake drawing her attention. "Oh! I've caught a fish!" she exclaimed. After much pulling and shrieking on her part, Trey finally took the pole and in one swift move, was holding up her fish, all three inches of it.

He raised an eyebrow at her. "Think this will feed us tonight?" He removed the hook and handed the fish to Lucy. She cried and moved away quickly. He laughed and released the fish back into the lake. "Grow a little more first, little fish," he said.

Lucy laughed at his antics. After he baited her hook again and handed the pole to her, he resumed his prone position. She watched him for a few moments and realized that the strained appearance he had been wearing seemed to have faded slightly. She signed and leaned back on her elbows beside him.

Trey was transfixed on his line recalling how he failed his father's last request by not taking care of Saphronia. He searched his mind over and over for a bit of wisdom his father had relayed to him that might help him in this situation. How to fix it. How to correct everything, so that he could keep his promise.

They continued to sit in silence for thirty minutes or more. Something inside Lucy told her Trey needed the quiet, and so she merely enjoyed the fresh air and sunshine. Trey's thoughts continued down memory lane, appreciating the recollections of his father. He recalled arriving home after the carriage accident and his father's valet, Matthew, had met him at the door.

He sighed. "Father didn't die right away in the accident," he broke the silence.

Lucy's head turned quickly to him trying to make certain she had heard him correctly. His expression had not changed as he watched his line dangling in the water. "I did not know that," she commented quietly.

He pursed his lips tightly and went back to his silent retreat. "When I returned home after getting the news, Father's valet told me that Father had survived for an hour. His last words were 'Tell Trey he must take care of Saphornia,'"

"He would be very proud of you, Trey," she soothed.

Trey snorted. "I didn't do a very good job. I can't see Father being happy that I allowed his little girl to be ruined by a scoundrel who will destroy her eventually."

Lucy wanted to remind him that he was ruining her just as well should this misadventure be known to society, but she held her tongue on that thought. "Perhaps if he were still here, your father would not be pleased with the way things happened, but I do not believe he would feel you have failed to care for your sister."

He shifted positions and sat up, laying his pole down beside his long legs. He folded his arms across his bent knees. "I don't see how he couldn't be."

Lucy set her pole down and rested her hand on top of his. "Trey, many young men in your position would have shuffled their younger siblings off to a distant relative and forgotten about them except for an occasional visit or holiday. My goodness, I have friends whose own parents sent them off to get them out of their hair. You did not do that. You cared for her, kept her with you, and gave her a secure home."

He rested his face on his folded arms and thought about her words. He had been determined to do everything right by his sister, and he thought he had done just that. He had prevented his friends from calling at his home socially when Saphronia was present to protect her from their roughness. Perhaps that had been a mistake.

Saphronia had spent the past year with an aunt learning the finer points of society for her social debut. Trey had gone to visit her several times a month because he missed her being around. He had never thought that she was underfoot or a damper to his life. She was his world.

He took a deep breath as he raised his head and picked up his pole. He gave her a boyish grin. "Are you sorry I talked you into coming with me to fish?"

She chuckled. "Well, we don't seem to be having much success catching our supper."

Now it was Trey's turn to chuckle. "Fishing isn't always about catching fish," he explained.

"You seem more relaxed here than I've seen you since, well..." She ended her sentence. The last thing she wanted to do was remind him of how angry he was with Jack.

"That's why I fish. I can relax. I think about my father and how he would handle situations that I am dealing with at the time. Somehow it always makes me feel better." He stopped suddenly and looked away. "I've never told anybody that. I don't know why I said it."

Lucy placed her hand on his back for support. "Sometimes it helps to talk. I think you're very fortunate to have such a therapeutic outlet."

There was something in her voice that seemed so sad that Trey swung his head to look at her. "Oh?" he said not certain how to proceed.

She smiled weakly. "I just mean, I wish I had somebody to talk to about Father. Mother gets so sad, and Jack just shrugs it off. I sometimes feel all alone. There are nights when I sneak down and sit in his study and try to remember every detail of him. I'm afraid that with each passing day, I'll forget part of those details."

Trey gave her an encouraging look. "I'll make you a promise. Anytime you wish to talk about your father, I am more than happy to oblige."

"Thank you. That is very kind of you," she stated. She was seeing a side of Trey that she had not noticed before. Trey was the charmer, the social darling, the doting brother, the scandal-free earl. He always appeared to have it all together. Perhaps he was human after all.

The earl sighed and turned back to his fishing line. He had not only shocked himself by spilling his secrets to Lucy, but he was even more amazed at how much better she made him feel. She understood what it was like to lose a father and to need to talk about the emotions that surrounded such a tragic event.

"I think I might go inside now if you don't mind," she said.

"Are you alright? Have I bored you so quickly?"

She chuckled. "Of course not. I would just like to get out of the sun. "

He jumped to his feet and reached to assist her. "I'm sorry. I should have brought a shade to protect you."

She took his proffered hand and rose gracefully. "Next time," she answered grinning up at him.

Trey couldn't help holding her hand just a bit too long as he gazed longer than was acceptable into her eyes. He felt himself being pulled towards her, and he shivered, breaking the spell that had come over them. "Right. Next time," he replied.

Lucy lowered her eyes and nodded as he released her hands. Slowly she turned and walked away wondering why she had never thought about this side of Trey before. Perhaps she had never imagined any man could feel such deep emotions. She took a relaxing breath. She had to stick to her plan. Keep him off balanced so she could convince him to give up and take her home. She could not let her emotions get involved.

The earl's eyes could not stop watching the gentle sway of her hips as she walked back to the house. He swallowed hard as he felt his body once again react to her. Damn! This was not to be! Why was he reacting so to her? It had been many years since a woman had left him so rattled, and he wasn't quite sure how to handle it now.

Lucy sat at the dressing table brushing her hair as she prepared for bed that night. She had spent the afternoon looking over his library until supper. Trey seemed rather quiet during their meal and afterward had excused himself with the pretext of needing to visit the stables. She had returned to the library thinking he would eventually join her, but as the hour grew later, Lucy had decided to retire.

The door opened and snapped her out of her thoughts.

Trey's eyes moved to the bed when he entered. Seeing it empty, he quickly scanned the room and was relieved when he noticed her sitting at the dressing table. She was brushing her long golden hair but had stopped upon spying him in the mirror, brush in mid stroke. Trey felt as if he had just intruded on the intimate act of her readying herself for bed, but all he could see was her full breasts exposed just above the neckline of a pink silk negligee.

Even when she stood up and turned towards him, he was unable to make himself speak. This gown was more provocative than the others, and he wondered if she realized it. Her sheer robe was hanging open revealing a high slit up the side of the gown with each step she took. He swallowed and cleared his throat to find his voice.

"I thought you would already be in bed," he finally managed to get out.

She walked toward him, noticing his face flush as she neared him. At the last second, she stepped around him and stood next to the bed. "I was just woolgathering and lost track of time," she replied as she shrugged out of the robe, arching her back in the process.

Trey groaned. Surely, she didn't realize what she was doing. The material was gathered just beneath her breasts, accenting them more than he needed to see. He turned away and walked to the window willing his body to cool. He heard her climb in the bed and listened to the sounds of her settling down. It took several long moments before he was able to turn around.

He found the stack of pillows they used as a barrier between them each night and placed them in the middle of the bed. He could feel her watching him, but he would not look up. When that was finished he sat down on his side of the bed and stretched out. He reached over and extinguished the light.

"Thank you for taking me fishing today," she said breaking the silence.

"Thank you for joining me. I rather enjoyed it." And he truly did enjoy her company even though it still surprised him.

The silence returned. Lucy had thought he had avoided her because of his confession today, so she wasn't certain if he was telling the truth or merely being polite.

Trey's thoughts drifted back to their conversation at the lake, and there was something he still didn't understand. "Lucy," he called softly. "Do you know why Sophie won't talk to me about Mother and Father?"

Lucy exhaled. "I think she feels she would be betraying you if she did."

"How?" he asked in shock. "That doesn't make any sense."

Without thinking she reached over and took his hand. "You have been responsible for her longer than your parents. Her loyalty to you is strong. Perhaps she feels that if she mentions them, you would feel that she doesn't appreciate what you have done for her."

"She won't talk about them for fear of hurting my feelings?" he asked in disbelief.

Lucy squeezed his hand for reassurance. "She loves you. And she was very young when they died. Although she loves them, her source of security changed from your parents to you. She feels that she must only be loyal to you now."

Guilt washed over Trey. He had never imagined that Saphronia was trying to protect his feelings when she claimed not to want to talk about their parents. "I feel like an ass now," he stated.

She leaned up on one elbow. "Please don't, Trey," she begged. "She loves you so much and thinks she is sparing your feelings. Perhaps it is also her way of dealing with the loss."

Trey squeezed her hand for support. "You are correct. How on earth did you get to be so insightful, Lucy?" he chuckled softly. His thumb stroked across her own in a seductive caress.

Lucy's heart rate increased at his action. She felt flutters in her stomach at his touch. She had never experienced such a sensation, but she liked it. It was as if he were making her a promise of something more without saying anything.

"Goodnight, Lucy," he whispered, but still he kept hold of her hand, stroking and caressing her skin until he fell asleep.

Chapter Five

A week had passed, and the boredom had reached a boiling point with Lucy. Trey had joined her for meals and then seemingly disappeared until the next meal. Lucy was certain that he was struggling to continue with this charade and thought it wouldn't be long before he took her home. Instead, he avoided her. That morning at breakfast she had voiced her monotony with her routine, and Trey shocked her by inviting her to go swimming in the lake.

Trey was already in the lake's warm water when Lucy approached. She watched him floating on his back as if he hadn't a care in the world and smiled. This was the Trey she enjoyed. The Trey who could be so intense, so serious, and yet on that rare occasion when he let his worries go, so wonderful. "Is the water warm?" she called out to him.

Trey was startled from his own thoughts by her voice and dropped his legs down until he was bobbing in the water. He glanced up and saw her attire and laughed. "What are you wearing?" Her dress was just plain ugly and hung on her in a most unflattering way.

Lucy glared at him. "Since I wasn't given time to pack a proper swimming dress, I borrowed one from Mrs. Grouse."

Trey covered his amused expression quickly and nodded. "And you look lovely," he noted. And truthfully, she did. If you just looked at her face and her hair braided in a single plait down her back and removed the dress. No! Trey moaned softly. He should have never thought of removing that dress.

Lucy removed her slippers and stuck a toe into the water to test its temperature. Trey noted the lovely curve of her ankle and calf as she raised her skirt just slightly. He took a deep breath and shook his head. Lucy made a half step into the lake but suddenly squealed and jumped back.

"What's wrong?" Trey called. He knew the water wasn't cold although he quite wished it were an ice bath at the moment to cool off his lust for a female he had no business lusting after.

"It's muddy and well, icky," she answered as she looked around trying to find a better place to enter.

"Run and you won't it feel it for long," he prompted. When he realized that she wasn't about to put her feet back in the mud willingly, he swallowed a grumbled retort and made his way toward her. He walked out of the water, shirtless, and revealing his broad chest and heavily muscled arms, water dripping off him.

Lucy swallowed for some reason. Good Lord, she had never seen a man this handsome and so, well, undressed. She glanced down at his pants, which were cut off at his knees and revealed his lower legs and bare feet. It seemed so intimate. Before she could recover, she found herself swept up in his arms and carried into the lake.

They had gone a few feet when Trey tossed her forward. "Don't put your feet down yet if you don't want to feel the mud," he teased.

Lucy floated on her back but managed to throw a handful of water in his direction which made him laugh. He dove under the water's surface and came up just past her, slicing through the lake with smooth even strokes. Lucy watched the muscles in his bare back work. My, he was beautiful.

"Are you coming or not?" he called from ten feet away. Lucy smiled and swam toward him. Trey dunked underwater and popped right back up wiping the water from his face before shaking the water from his hair. "You won't be feeling any mud here."

Lucy let her feet fall and touched the muddy bottom. She let out a shriek and glared at him. He threw his head back in laughter. "That wasn't funny!" she scolded but even she wasn't immune to his good humor today. She playfully swam away adding an extra kick with her feet to splash him.

Trey followed her and the two enjoyed the water for several long silent minutes. Lucy looked around the woods and hills surrounding the lake and sighed. "It is beautiful here," she said softly.

"Yes, it is," he answered and surveyed the scenery. "I've always enjoyed this place. It's peaceful. Makes the rest of the world not seem to matter."

She smiled at his description. "It's funny, but I feel like I've been here before." She turned and casually asked, "Where are we?"

Trey froze. He didn't think she had ever been to this hunting lodge, but the lake was connected to her brother's manor house on the other end several miles away. He knew the family hadn't been here for years, but he now realized that the landscape might stir up memories of Lucy's childhood. "My hideout," he teased hoping to stop her questioning.

As if on queue, she screamed and flung herself right at him. Trey was barely touching the bottom of the lake when she wrapped her arms and legs around him and tried to climb even higher.

When he recovered from his shock, he found his hands had instinctively cradled her bare bottom while the skirt floated upward in the lake. Dear Lord, she was soft and curvaceous there, he thought and then wanted to kick himself as his manhood realized the same thing and sprang to life.

Lucy finally ceased her squawking enough for Trey to decipher a fish touched her ankle. She lifted her head from the crook of his neck. When she leaned back with her hands resting lightly on his shoulders and her legs were still locked behind his back, his eyes drifted to the water line where her breasts bobbed dangerously close to slipping out of that awful much-too-large-for-her dress. His staff was now at full attention.

Tearing his gaze from her bosom, his eyes lifted to her face and her full lips, slightly parted. He swallowed and tried to think of something other than this beautiful woman scandalously clinging to him. He licked his lips to try to make them work. "When did you turn into such a female?" His words were low and husky although he'd meant them to be teasing and light. He cleared his throat.

"A female? What do you mean?" she asked and adorably cocked her head at him.

He grinned. "The worms are icky. The lake is muddy. A fish touched my ankle." His voice was high pitched as he mocked her. She blushed, and he instantly knew he had to taste her, kiss her, release her breasts from that ugly excuse of a dress, and explore her entire body with his hands, his lips, his tongue. But instead, he growled and threw her away from him.

The shock of his actions found Lucy sinking like a rock until she recovered her senses and came up laughing, sputtering and finally throwing water at him. She moved around behind him attempting to dunk him and not realizing that her breasts had now escaped the dress and were pressing against his bare broad back. She heard him groan slightly before spinning around and clutching her hands.

Unable to use her hands to stay above water, she again locked her legs around his middle as she wrestled with him to free her hands, both giggling and laughing. When she finally succeeded, her face was a breath from Trey's. His eyes burned into her own with something she couldn't quite understand but knew she desperately wanted to know more. His heated gaze stopped her laughter, and he continued to study her for several quiet moments.

Abruptly he lost all sense of control and moved his head forward just a fraction of an inch until his lips met hers. Soft, tender, and innocently intoxicating. He gently stroked and let his tongue explore the delicate outline of her lush lips. So sweet and enticing. He lifted his head and tried to find the words to say how sorry he was. But even as the idea entered his mind, he knew the words would be a lie.

A slight smile formed on Lucy's angelic face making Trey feel even worse. Before he could change this scene, Lucy leaped up and pushed his head underwater. When he resurfaced, she was giggling at him but seeing the shock in his eyes, she quickly squealed and swam away from him.

Trey caught her in three strokes. "You little minx!" He charged as laughter bubbled out of him. She turned back to face him, smiling innocently until she pushed forward and kissed him. Trey froze as she bobbed against him. He let her explore his own lips and when one of her hands cupped the side of his face, he thought he would be undone. She lifted her head and when she looked at him, she blushed prettily at her own boldness. Trey let his fingers stroke the side of her face, down her neck, until they reached her shoulder. And then he dunked her and darted away.

And so began their game. Dunking, swimming away and then a simple sweet kiss when the dunker was caught. Nothing more. Just innocent play Trey continued to tell himself, but with each kiss, each touch, he was finding himself wanting to show her more and more. After an hour, Trey lifted her in his arms and carried her out of the lake, each laughing over their fun afternoon in the water.

He knelt down and set her gently on the ground, but when he attempted to stand, she held onto his arm and pulled him down over her. With her free hand, she laid it against his bare chest. "Thank you for today," she whispered.

One last kiss, Trey decided. He moved over her and captured her lips with his own. The kiss started as innocent as the others, but when he heard her desirous moan, he deepened it just a bit. Lucy gasped and her lips parted. Trey could not help but accept the invitation she did not realize she had just issued to him and tentatively probed his hot tongue between her open lips. She opened more and was soon meeting his tongue with her own, exploring this new sensation with innocent reactions.

Trey's hand moved to her neck and slaked lower and lower but just before he reached his goal, his senses recovered. He ended the kiss and still hovered over her. "Lucy, you should go inside now." His voice was soft and low, not angry, not scolding. Just defeated. "Please," he added.

Confusion filled her eyes, but she rose and returned to the house. When she entered their bedroom she walked over to the mirror and looked at her reflection. Surely she must look different now after that kiss. Her first kiss! She must have changed in some way. Her lips were red and a bit swollen, but other than that, she saw no changes. She sighed and rang for a bath.

Trey pulled up the borrowed mount at the top of a hill overlooking the hunting lodge. He could not believe he had kissed Lucy, and even more, he could not believe the passionate response she had given. What had happened? This was not part of his carefully thought out plans. He would have to avoid her more than he had been. He could not take a chance of a repeat encounter.

He dismounted from the horse and sat on the ground watching the lodge, wondering what Lucy was doing at this moment. She was probably dressing for supper. He could see the light coming from the dining room and could picture her face upon learning that she would be dining alone. He pushed down the guilty impulse that almost made him join her, but he couldn't take the chance. He had to keep his distance.

As the hours passed, he watched the light fill their bedroom. *Their bedroom?* The very idea of those words sent a shiver down his spine. It was her room, and he was just staying there to make sure she didn't leave. Because if she wondered outside here, she could get lost or hurt or somebody could find her and then she would be in a dangerous position. He repeated this thought over and over as if to justify his reasoning for sleeping in her bed.

Lucy. Even as he thought of her, she stood in the bedroom window, silhouetted by the light from within the room. She would be wearing one of those damn negligees, and he could picture her in it now. The cool silk hanging loosely about her, ending mid-thigh and exposing the rest of her shapely legs. God, she had beautiful legs.

He moaned as he recalled those legs wrapped around him today, and he was instantly hard. He could have sunk himself into her, and she would have clung to him, let him do whatever he wanted. And right now, he wanted to teach her everything he knew about passion and desire. She was so receptive, so desirable, and her body! He knew, he just *knew*, she was a perfect fit for him. Her legs, her arms, her breasts, her bottom. There was nothing he would change about her.

His manhood throbbed painfully now against his ever-tightening breeches. With a primal growl, he tore open the buttons containing himself. He took his rod in his own hand and began to ease the need. He closed his eyes against what he had resorted to, but that was his downfall.

With his eyes closed, he could feel her legs wrapped around him, he could see her breasts bobbing right in front of him in the water, he could savor the touch of her rounded bottom nestled in his hands, and he could taste her sweet kisses. The last thought sent him over the edge with a strangled cry to silence the release that he so desperately needed.

Collapsing on his back, Trey stared up at the moon, and he for some reason he recalled his mother telling him about the man in the moon when he was a child. He chuckled. If there was a man in the moon, he must certainly be sorry for the show he had just witnessed.

Lucy woke early the next morning, and the first thing she noticed was an arm draped across her waist and a very male body spooned against her backside. Every instinct in her body told her to turn towards him, but after his reaction to yesterday afternoon, she felt that he would turn and run. Instead, she enjoyed the feeling of his arm around her and pretended to sleep.

Trey woke cradled tightly to Lucy's curves. Carefully, so as not to wake her, he slid his arm from around her waist and sat up. He looked down on her sleeping form. Her golden hair was spread across the pillow, a stray strand had fallen over her face. He reached out and moved it from her cheek. She looked so beautiful in rest. His lips turned up in a small smile, and he leaned down and kissed her soft cheek. She sighed but did not wake, and he thought her even more perfect than before.

Chapter Six

James entered the Dowager Duchess of Brighton's sitting room with a grim expression. Isabelle was reading aloud to Jack's mother in a low soft voice. The older lady was staring straight ahead as if in a daze and not really listening to Isabelle. He quietly cleared his throat.

Isabelle glanced up at the doorway. "James," she whispered softly and then blushed as she realized her mistake. She cleared her throat and closed the book. "Kettering," she tried again.

James nodded at her and walked straight to the dowager. He kneeled before her and took her hands. "Your Grace, have you any news?" It was the same question he had asked her for weeks each time he visited.

Lila Cavanaugh turned to face James as if she were in a trance. She stared at him before letting out a long breath and shaking her head. "Nothing. Not a word."

Moments after Jack and Sophie had departed from their wedding, the dowager was presented with a missive that simply said, "I would never harm her." It wasn't until an hour later when the house had been turned upside down and Lucy was nowhere to be found, that they started to piece it all together. Not wanting to draw attention to the matter, only their small group was aware of what had happened.

Lila Cavanaugh had insisted that Jack not be informed. She was certain that Trey would realize his error and return her daughter within a day or two. When three days had come and gone with no sign of Trey or Lucy, the word was put out that Lucy had returned to the country for a visit with a great aunt.

In the days that had followed, James, Parker, and Kit had ventured out to each of Trey's homes and estates. One by one, they returned with no sign of Trey. The ladies, Isabelle, Anna, and Julia had taken turns keeping the dowager company and reassuring her that Trey would never hurt Lucy. But Lila did not need to be told that. She knew in her heart that Trey would keep her safe physically.

It was the threat to her innocent daughter's reputation that worried her. Society would destroy Lucy should the truth ever get out. She took a deep breath. It was time to stop feeling sorry for herself and to take charge of this situation. She knew that if she let go of her worry, she could figure out where Trey had gone.

And although she meant well, listening to Isabelle read to her was not going to help her clear her mind. "I believe I will lay down for a while," she announced and stood up.

James stumbled backward from his crouched position and quickly rose. Isabelle jumped up to take the dowager's arm, but Lila shook her assistance away. "I'll be fine. You should go home and enjoy yourself. I don't need a nursemaid at my age," she stated firmly.

They were a bit taken aback by her change in demeanor but at the same time, they were pleased to see her strong spirit emerge. James bowed politely as the older woman swept out of the room.

Isabelle followed her to the door and watched as she made her way down the hall to the stairs. She stood there for a few moments before turning around.

"Well," she started.

James shook his head and chuckled. "She's quite amazing."

"She's been so dejected and sad. I almost think it's more painful to her that Trey did this," she noted. When James raised an eyebrow at her, she continued. "She knows, as we both do, that Trey would never harm Lucy."

James flopped down in a chair and looked up at the ceiling. Isabelle was humored at his informal behavior but decided not to chastise him for it. It had been a stressful two weeks for all of them. She crossed to a matching chair and sat down.

The mantle clock ticked away as they both sat in silence trying to once again understand what in the world the earl was thinking in this scheme. He had been furious over Jack and Sophie's relationship, but to take it this far was beyond anything they could have imagined.

Finally, Isabelle cleared her throat. "Do you think he realized what would happen by stealing a young lady away like this?"

James scowled and shook his head. "Not at first. I think he was perhaps so blinded by his anger that he wasn't thinking of the repercussions."

"And now?"

He snorted. "And now whether he realizes it or not, he's walked into his own parson's trap. Poor fool."

Isabelle glared at him. "Poor Trey? What about poor Lucy? She's the innocent party in all of this and is now going to be linked to him for the rest of her life. He took away all of her dreams and hopes with his own selfish actions!"

James leaned over and placed his hand on top of hers. "I didn't mean to lessen her situation. And despite his idiotic behavior, Trey will be good to her."

She sighed. "You don't understand at all. He stole her chance to fulfill her dreams. But most men don't care if a woman has a plan of their own. A woman's sole purpose is to do what men think is best for her, right?"

James was quickly on his knees before her, holding her small hand in his large one. "You know that I don't feel that way. Have I not always supported you for sticking to your own plans and dreams? Why would I want any lady to give up her own dreams?"

Isabelle lowered her eyes. "I know," she answered quietly. "But it just seems that everybody is looking at this as if Trey is the one who will be making a sacrifice by doing the right thing."

"You are correct, as usual," he said with a supportive grin. "Perhaps it's because I relate more to the male view of issues than to the female view. Although I try my best to understand, I sorely lack in the experience to do so."

She raised her face to meet his gaze. "I suppose I cannot fault you for what you have never been nor ever will be." And then her expression returned to all seriousness. "James, do you think they will do well together? I don't know Chelmsworth very well, but I've always heard good things."

James chuckled and shook his head. "Society's darling," he snorted and shook his head. "You ladies sure think highly of our young earl."

Her eyes widened. "You mean he is not a gentleman?" Her heart sank at the thought of Lucy being locked in an unhappy match.

"Of course, he is a gentleman through and through," he quickly answered. "Trey is, well, Trey." He returned to his chair. "What of Lady Lucinda?"

"What of her?" Isabelle snapped in return.

He shrugged. "I don't know her well. Is she a good person?"

Isabelle smiled as she thought of her friend. "She is. She was so excited for her come out, more so than the rest of us ever thought of being. And not to find a husband, but to experience all of the aspects of society that had only been hinted to her before."

"She wanted the whole grand season, eh?" he chuckled. "And Trey has drastically altered her plans. Poor girl."

"Who's a poor girl?" a voice called from the doorway.

Isabelle and James both turned to find Anna standing in the doorway. "We were discussing Lucy," Isabelle explained.

"Any word?" the newcomer inquired. When both parties shook their heads, she sighed. "Poor girl is right." She turned to Isabelle. "Parker is waiting to take you home."

Isabelle sighed and stood up. "Very well. Just so you know the Dowager is getting annoyed with us being underfoot. She's retreated to her room to get away."

"I'll see you out," James said and helped Isabelle to her feet. He nodded at Anna and escorted Isabelle from the room.

After seeing her into the waiting carriage and exchanging a few words with Parker, he decided he was not at all prepared to go home. Perhaps if he went to his club, he might hear something, anything that might lead them to Trey's whereabouts.

Thirty minutes later he entered the gentleman's club and found a quiet table in the corner where he could see and hear the happenings around him. He had just been served a drink and placed it to his lips when a man sat down across from him.

"Kettering," the Earl of Lowdes greeted.

James looked up. "Lowdes," he returned dryly.

"I've seen you a lot in my neighborhood of late," he commented. When James' eyes narrowed in confusion, he continued. "My new neighbor moved in just before her only son married."

James cringed. Damn! He had forgotten that Jack's mother had recently purchased the home next to Jason Havers, the Earl of Lowdes. "I'll remember to stop by for tea the next time I am in the area," James countered.

Jason chuckled. "Heard Lady Lucinda is visiting an aunt. Funny time to up and leave in the middle of the season. My sister was very excited to be neighbors with her friend and the two had talked non-stop over this season."

James shrugged. "A lady can change her mind."

The earl took a drink from his glass and studied the duke over the rim. "Touché." He continued to watch James until he lowered his glass. "Where's Chelmsworth been keeping himself?"

It took every ounce of control James could muster to not react to the bait being tossed his way. He *knew*! Somehow, someway, Lowdes knew that Trey had taken off with Lucy. He didn't have any personal issues with this man, but he knew that Jack and Jason had battled back and forth for years over one thing or another. He shrugged. "I don't keep tabs on him. Have you checked his home?"

Lowdes shook his head and then downed the rest of his drink. He stood and rested his hands on the back of the chair. "Perhaps he is looking over the old hunting lodge up north that he just bought from me."

James' head snapped up at that. "What did you say?"

A sly knowing smile crossed the earl's rugged face. "He's hinted about it for years, but strangely became quite insistent on it lately. I finally gave in."

"What lodge is this?" James demanded, forgetting about trying to hide his feelings.

"Near to Brighton's old ancestral home. He doesn't get up there very often being so far from town. Our fathers used to take us there for some hunting and fishing when we were lads." He stood up straight and adjusted his jacket. "Stop by for a visit, the next time you're in my neighborhood. By your recent habits, that should be tomorrow early morning, correct?" He chuckled as he walked away.

James waited until he was certain Jason Havers had left. Then he shoved away from the table and quickly made his own exit. He had to tell the dowager, but it was too late to do so tonight. Damn, Lowdes! Hopefully, he was correct, and they could find Trey before Jack got his hands on him.

The next morning James was knocking on the Dowager Duchess of Brighton's home before it was anywhere near an acceptable time to pay a social call. He noticed her carriage standing in front of the home and was wondering what it was doing there this early when the door opened, and Julia stood on the other side.

"James!" she exclaimed in surprise at the same time he was saying "Julia!"

"Thank God you are here," she added and pulled her brother inside the home shutting the door quickly. "She insists on going north to Brighton Hall. I tell you, she is not behaving normally!"

James' eyes widened. "Has Lowdes been here?"

Julia shook her head. "Not that I know of, but you are not listening to me! She is taking off to the country when Lucy is still missing."

"Where is the dowager?" James asked pushing past his sister and heading towards the stairs. He paused at the foot and looked back at Julia.

"She's in her sitting room writing notes before she leaves."

James bounded up the stairs three at a time and rushed along the hall realizing he wasn't quite sure where the dowager's sitting room was located. Glancing in each door as he made his way through her home, he finally located the correct room.

"Your Grace," he called breathlessly. "Have you any news?"

Lila Cavanaugh looked up. "No, but I have a very strong feeling," she answered warmly.

"Trey bought the hunting lodge near Brighton Hall just recently," he blurted out.

A smile slowly formed across the older lady's face. "My intuition was correct then." She gathered up the notes she had been writing and rose elegantly. She crossed towards James and handed him the notes. "You may deliver these before you follow."

He looked down at the correspondence he now held wondering why he was being reassigned as a footman. "What are these?"

She patted his cheek as she passed by. "Why, invitations. What else?" She swept out of the room and James was left stunned by her nonchalant behavior. He quickly regained his composure and rushed out after her.

He caught up to her at the bottom of the stairs where she was directing her footman with her luggage. "Be careful with that. As a matter of fact, I want that inside the carriage with me," she scolded nodding towards a large dress box. She turned around and looked at James. "And yes, I've already sent a message to my son."

"James, what is going on?" Julia whispered.

He shook his head. "I don't know how she figured it out, but she's going after her daughter."

Jack bent over and kissed Sophie's sleeping form. His heart soared as it did every single time he looked at his wife. *His wife*! Not so long ago he would have sworn marriage would never catch him by surprise, and now he could not imagine how he would ever survive without Sophie. Even as he walked out of the room, he could not stop smiling.

His smile was still wide as he passed a maid in the hall and nodded to her. Trey may have pushed him into this wedding trip, but he was truly happy he had agreed. Spending time alone with Sophie had been perfect without society breathing down their necks or some pressing matter pulling him away. He had left specific instructions that only dire matters be brought to his attention. His estate managers could handle everything else.

He strolled into the study to read the morning paper, as was his habit until Sophie awoke for breakfast. He reached for the paper waiting on the desk and noticed a letter resting on top of it. Taking both he sat down in a chair and opened the letter first.

A single piece of parchment was inside. He held it up and his heart stopped. *Your sister for mine.* The message was short but clear. Jack roared his anger and stood up. He would kill him. When he found Trey Harrow, he would kill him with his bare hands. Throwing the paper across the room, he stormed out of the room barking orders to the servants as he stomped upstairs to wake his wife.

Chapter Seven

Lucy's eyes fluttered open in the morning and shivered at the chill in the room despite the closeness of a male body beside her.

"Are you cold?" Trey asked in a husky tone of one who had just awakened. He pulled her closer to him and wrapped his arms around her. "Better?"

Lucy nodded and sighed as she enjoyed the feel of him so close to her. She was well aware that they had moved beyond any acceptable behavior and had reached a dangerous level. She was already ruined morally, having been alone with a man for weeks now, but emotionally she was finding herself drawn closer and closer to Trey.

Each evening as they settled into bed, they would lay awake and talk. Never about Jack or the reason they were now in this situation. Trey held her gently and sometimes he would kiss her, and Lucy found herself almost pleading for more of the unknown. But in those moments, Trey would pull away and leave her wondering what she was missing.

"What are your plans for today?" he asked as he did each morning.

Lucy wanted to be sarcastic in her response, but she could not risk losing the ground she had made so far. She felt that at any day he would realize he had to return her to her mother. But as each day passed, she felt no desire to leave him. She was learning so much about this man that she had never imaged.

"I suppose I'll work on your library lists. Did you know there isn't a single play on the shelves?" she turned her head towards him.

"Is that bad?" he asked as his lips found the crook of her neck.

"Every library has a collection of plays. Do you have any requests for that list?" she asked as her breath caught from the sensation his lips and tongue were sending through her.

He chuckled. "No. I trust your judgment." He drew her earlobe between his lips and nibble on it lightly with his teeth.

Lucy spun towards him and leaned over. "You don't have a favorite?" He shrugged. "But I thought you loved the theater? Jack said you attended several times a week."

Trey's smile faded and a slight blush covered his face. "I, uh..."

And then it hit Lucy. The lady on stage who had been staring at Trey during the performance she and Jack had with Trey and Sophie. The beautiful woman had stared intently at Trey as if she knew him personally. Intimately. "That lady," she started. "She's your mistress," she accused and sat up quickly.

Trey reached to pull her back to him. "I have no mistress," he stated before covering her lips with his own. His kiss coaxed and tempted her to enjoy the moment and forget everything else. It worked for a few moments until she sat up in bed again and moved away from him.

"Several times a week," she whispered. She stared at him in shock. "And I suppose I am just a substitute until you can return to your regular routine." She threw back the covers and stood up.

It took Trey a few moments to realize what she was saying. He shook his head and reached for her hand. "No, Lucy. You are not a substitute." He held onto her hand and crawled towards her, pulling her back up onto the bed and into his arms. "You are not a substitute, and I'm sorry if I've made you feel that way."

He held her tightly against him, resting his head on the top of hers. He didn't want to hurt her, and he had never imagined he would enjoy her company so well. But it had never crossed his mind to use her.

She struggled to remove herself from his grip. "No!" she cried and pushed herself away from his arms. "You and your secret sordid life think to use me for your pleasure. Was this planned as well? As part of your revenge on Jack? Dally with his sister? Laugh at him behind his back? Laugh at me?" She swallowed the lump in her throat to stop the tears that threatened.

Trey was on his feet in an instant. "No, please. I had no intentions of ever hurting you or using you."

"Please, just get out," she choked out. "I want to dress." She turned her back to him. She felt betrayed all over again, and she didn't want to face him. The silence grew louder, and the walls seemed to close in around her, she waited. Finally, she heard the door open and close, and she let out a heavy breath. She turned back to make certain he was gone.

A part of her hurt that he had walked out instead of trying to convince her that she had it wrong. But a part of her just wanted to be as far away from him as possible. She could not concentrate on anything when he was this close except how much she enjoyed his kisses and his embraces.

After washing and dressing, she waited by the window until she saw Trey stalking off towards the stable. She had no idea what he did out there all day but she never heard a horse leave. He stayed away until supper, sometimes not even coming back in for that. And she was left alone, wondering these halls and rooms trying to find something to occupy her time.

Her anger grew as she made her way downstairs. She was going to find out what he was up to. Find out why he was avoiding her during the day and then holding her so close at night. As she reached the bottom of the stairs, she stopped. No! She would not go to him.

She heard laughter coming from the kitchen and decided to visit with Mrs. Grouse. The housekeeper was always welcoming and seemed to understand Lucy's predicament. She smiled at the thought of the pleasant older woman and made her way towards the housekeeper's domain.

"My lady!" the housekeeper said in surprise. "I did not know you were awake. My lord has not rang for his breakfast yet, and I just assumed you were still abed." She laid down the knife and apple she had been holding and quickly busied herself at the stove. "I'll have your breakfast ready in just a jiffy."

"No worries," Lucy replied. "I'm not really hungry this morning."

Mrs. Grouse moved quickly to the lady's side. "Are you unwell, my lady?" she asked with motherly concern.

"Oh, I feel fine," she answered. "I just, well, I'm just not hungry is all." She glanced down to hide the tears she could feel welling up in her eyes.

"Ah," the housekeeper stated with understanding on her face. "Would you like to have a seat and keep me company then?" she asked and nodded to a stool next to her work table.

Lucy managed a weak smile and took a seat. "I suppose that you don't know where Lord Chelmsworth has taken himself off to this morning?"

Mrs. Grouse shook her head as she returned to her work. "No, I've not seen him and thought he was still abed. Would you like me to send Matthew to find him?"

"Oh no! Don't do that!" she cried out and then quickly blushed. "I mean, I wouldn't want to bother him."

"Of course not." The housekeeper poured a glass of milk and set it on the table without comment.

"You see, I don't have any right or expectation to know of Chelmsworth's comings and goings. Heavens, I should not even be here, but I am thankful for your presence as a chaperone." Her stomach growled loudly as the smells from the cookstove assaulted her nose.

"Of course, my lady," Mrs. Grouse answered and set a plate of eggs, ham, and toast on the table next to the milk. She walked to a cupboard and returned with a set of silverware that was shoved towards Lucy.

"And even if I did have that right, it's not as if a man would be expected to tell his plans," Lucy continued. Without thinking she reached for the silverware and began to eat the breakfast set before her.

Mrs. Grouse placed a pot of jam on the table and then leaned forward. "He would if he cared for you," she stated.

Lucy's fork froze in midair. Her eyes met the housekeeper's who was fixing her with a stoic stare. She returned her attention to her food. "Oh, but that is not the case with Trey."

A smile curved the lips of the older woman, and she turned away from her visitor. "I know it's not my place, but I believe you are wrong in your judgment, my lady."

She reached for the pot of jam and began slathering the fruity compote on her toast. "Nonsense. Trey does not look at me as anything except his means to revenge."

"If you say so, my lady."

Trey entered the house and didn't see anybody. His first thought was that Lucy had fled, but that was always his fear when she wasn't where he thought she should be. Lately, his fear wasn't so much that his plan for revenge on Jack would be ruined if she escaped, but he hated the idea of her just not being there with him. He shuddered. Why was he growing so comfortable with her?

He had let this part of his time with her get out of hand, and he was struggling each and every day to fight the feelings she invoked in him. Avoiding her during the day was easy, but today he had to face her again. He couldn't let her think that he had set out to seduce her, to ruin her, to take a temporary place of, well, one of the women he frequented. He had to make her understand that he would never use her in that way.

Voices coming from the kitchen drew his attention. He listened and picked up Lucy's light tones, and he relaxed. He made his way down towards the kitchen and stood in the open doorway. Lucy was nibbling on a piece of toast while Mrs. Grouse was busy at the stove. The housekeeper glanced up at him and nodded.

"My lord, is there something I can help you with?" she asked.

Lucy jumped up from her stool when she noticed him. "Oh!" she gasped and lost her balance.

Trey was across the room in a flash, grabbing her to keep from falling. When she had regained her balance, he removed his one hand from her waist but held her hand with his other. "Are you alright?" he asked softly, his eyes studying her face for any sign of distress.

"Thank you," she whispered, caught in the spell of his closeness. "I am fine."

He continued to hold her gaze and he could feel the pull of her, enticing him to kiss away that little drop of jam on her bottom lip. Her eyes widened slightly. He wondered if it was from fear or desire. He could not add to her distrust, and so he lifted a finger to her lip and wiped the sweet jam off. Her eyes followed his digit as he brought it to his lips and licked the sweetness off with a boyish grin.

Lucy's heart was racing at the intimate gesture and she wondered if he realized how it was affecting her. When he thread his fingers between hers, she glanced down at their joined hands, unsure what to say or do.

"Are you busy?" he asked. "I have a surprise for you." His voice was barely above a whisper as if he did not want anybody but herself to hear.

Lucy shook her head. "A surprise?"

He smiled warmly at her. "A surprise."

"What is it?" her voice full of curiosity.

He chuckled. "The point of a surprise is to not tell you until the surprise is revealed." He tucked a stray strand of hair behind her ear. "Can I steal you away for a bit?"

Lucy's pulsed raced at his touch and her breath caught in her throat. She swallowed and wet her lips. "Of course," she managed to get out.

Taking her by the hand he led her toward the back door. "Now close your eyes until I tell you to open them."

"Where are we going?" she asked.

"Tut, tut," he teased. "Now do as I say and close your eyes. I won't let you fall." He put his arm around her waist and held her close to his side. Lucy took unsure tiny steps afraid of what might be in her path. Trey chuckled. "Let's try it this way." The next thing Lucy knew she was being swept up in his arms. A squeal escaped her lips.

"Keep your eyes closed," he reminded.

"Where are you taking me?"

He chuckled. "Don't you trust me?"

Lucy snorted. "Trust the man who stole me from my family?"

Trey stopped, the smile quickly fading from his face until he noticed her teasing grin. He shifted her and held her close to his body. "You little minx." He resumed his steps for a few more minutes until he reached his destination. He carefully lowered her legs and let her slide down the length of him, holding her steady until she had regained her balance. "You can look now."

Lucy opened her eyes and realized they were standing beside the lake. And then she saw a small rowboat at the edge. Her head spun to Trey's and she stared at him wide-eyed. "That's a boat!"

"Very good. I always thought you were a smart one," he joked.

She rolled her eyes at his jest. "But where did you get it?"

Trey just smiled before scooping her back up and carrying her through the shallow water. He gently deposited her on the seat and then pushed the boat out into the lake until it floated freely, and he could jump in.

Once seated in the boat, he bent down and handed her a parasol. "To protect you from the sun," he announced with a flourish. Lucy smiled and took the item. He picked up the oars and began to row away from the bank. "Just sit back and enjoy your boat ride."

"Where on earth did you find a boat out in the middle of nowhere?" she inquired.

"I made it," he answered. "You said you would enjoy a boat ride on the lake."

Lucy's widened, and her heart stopped for a second. "You made this for me?" her voice full of shock.

Trey could feel his cheeks beginning to color, so he shrugged and looked away. "You and anybody else who wants to use it." He hoped he sounded casual. In truth, he had made it for her, but he felt silly admitting that.

"Oh," she said trying to hide the disappointment in his statement.

The earl had never wanted to kick himself so much in his life. He had hurt her again. He saw her delight disappear in an instant and he felt like an ass. "I wanted to make sure you were the first one to try it with me," he added and was relieved when she appeared pleased at his comment.

She settled back and enjoyed the swaying of the boat, the stillness that surrounded them, the way Trey's muscles tightened under his cambric shirt with each stroke. Her heart constricted as she recalled what was under that shirt, and she was suddenly warm.

"What do you think?" he asked and stopped rowing and leaned forward on the oars.

"It's beautiful, Trey. Is this where you were disappearing to every day?"

Trey smiled. "Yes. I'm sorry for being secretive, but I wanted to surprise you." He lowered his gaze to avoid her eyes. "It must have only added to your thinking my intentions were not honorable."

Now it was Lucy's turn to look away. "I'm sorry for accusing you of such," she whispered. "I am just..." Her words trailed off.

Trey's head snapped up to see what had happened. She was looking out over the lake to her side and biting her lower lip. "You're just what, Lucy?"

She sighed and turned back to face him. "I'm just confused as to why you would kiss me and hold me the way that you do. And then you seem to disappear as if you are angry with me." Her cheeks burned with embarrassment at asking such a bold question.

"Lucy, I, well, I..." he swallowed and took a deep breath. "I find myself attracted to you in a way that I should know better."

"Oh," she replied. She opened her mouth to speak again but could only repeat herself. "Oh." Did that mean he didn't want to be attracted to her?

He chuckled. "I've confused you. That's alright because I'm confused myself."

"Oh," she said for the third time.

"I had it in mind to borrow a little girl to get back at Brighton. A young girl that was the same age as my little sister."

"But we're not little girls," she pointed out.

He snorted. "Yes, I realize that now. Or rather I realized that rather early on in this scheme." He gave her his boyish grin. The smile faded and he looked at her with a serious stare. "But I never once thought to use you in a disrespectful way or for my own pleasure. Never, Lucy. I hope you believe me."

Lucy realized that he was telling the truth. His expression was pleading with her to believe him. She gave him a weak smile. "But if that wasn't your plan, what happened?"

"I told you. I can't help being attracted to you," he answered in a low husky voice. "I mean, look at you right now. You are absolutely beautiful with that green gown and that parasol perched over you. If I were a painter, I would certainly paint you in this setting."

She gasped at his words.

"You seem shocked," he noted.

"I've never imagined you to be a romantic."

He laughed. "Romantic or not, I speak the truth, my lady. You are breathtaking today."

Lucy turned away, not sure how to handle this conversation any longer. "You don't have to say that."

His laughter died leaving an awkward silence between them. "Lucy, it's the truth." He watched a pretty blush cover her smooth cheeks, and it brought him back to who she really was. He picked up the oars again. "Shall we head back now?"

That evening after supper, Trey joined Lucy in the library as she continued her list of what she felt he needed in the library. The earl was reclining in a comfortable leather chair with a glass of brandy and flipping through the pages of a book while Lucy scanned the shelves and made notes.

"Did you put together your own library at home?" he asked.

Lucy stopped her work and looked at him. "Not really. I've added a few recent publications, but my father was a great reader. The credit goes mostly to him."

Trey recalled the deceased Duke of Brighton reading by the fireplace each evening with his wife sitting in a matching chair sewing or doing needlepoint. A smile came to his face at the fond memory. "I remember that."

Lucy took a step towards him. "Jack enjoys reading as well." She waited for his reaction. She wanted more than anything for Trey to forget this hatred of her brother and so far he closed himself off when she attempted to bring Jack into the conversation.

Trey cocked his head and gave her a half smile. He knew what she was about. "Jack would not like it to be known that he spent many a night buried in a good book. It wouldn't help his reputation."

She released a breath. "Sophie enjoys reading as well. Perhaps they have more in common than you imagined."

He snorted. "Jack also enjoys drinking, gambling, whoring, and debauchery. I don't believe my sister enjoys those activities."

Lucy spun away from him as tears burned her eyes. How could she go from needing his nearness, his touch, and his kiss to wanting to never speak to him again? This would not work. Trey would forever blame her brother for falling in love with Sophie. Her tears had just started when she felt his presence right behind her.

"I'm sorry, Lucy," he said softly as his arms encircled her. "I should not have spoken to you that way."

Suddenly the anger she had been trying to suppress for weeks bubbled over. She twisted out of his arms and pushed away from him. "No!" she cried. "Do not touch me again!"

Trey froze and held his arms to his side.

"You dare point out Jack's faults as if you are not guilty of doing the same thing. But you neglected to mention a few of your own. While he and Sophie may have met under unusual circumstances, he fell in love with her, something you keep forgetting in your quest to villainize him."

He could not respond to her accusations. He was afraid that he would only hurt her even more, and so he remained silent.

"You were so determined to destroy my brother for your own selfish pride that you could care less that you have destroyed me in the process!" She stepped closer to him, one hand on her hip, the other pointing at his chest. "You could care less about my dreams, my hopes, or my plans! It's all about your devious desires to destroy two people who truly love one another all because it didn't happen as you planned it!"

He shook his head. It wasn't that way. Or was it? He knew he had hurt her, but he wasn't trying to destroy her. Just Jack.

The tears flowed freely from her eyes now. "Do you know what tomorrow is? I had vouchers to Almack's presented by Lady Jersey herself! Tomorrow was the dream I had been hoping for since I was a little girl, and you and your selfish behavior have just taken that away from me! You have ruined me, and I will never be afforded another chance!"

He stiffened. Her words cut like a knife. He reached for her, but she pushed his hands aside and rushed out of the room. Trey stood there with her words echoing inside his head, breaking his heart, and making him hate himself.

Chapter Eight

Once again Lucy awoke to the awareness of Trey's arms around her. She should be furious after crying herself to sleep over his selfishness. No, it wasn't as much over his selfishness as it was her own feelings for Trey.

She had always admired him and thought he was kind and polite, and society was head over heels in love with him. But she had suspected there had to be much more to him. Society always saw what they wanted to, and she knew from her own brother's experience that he was much more than the notorious rake most thought he was. Jack was loving and loyal and protective.

Trey was complex. He was full of anger but as Lucy listened to his words she had decided that he wasn't so much angry at Jack as he was at himself for what he thought was failing in providing his sister the perfect debut. Trey was consumed with fear that he would not live up to his image of his own father.

Lucy wasn't so much upset over missing out of Almack's as she was afraid of the feelings she was developing for him. And more than that, her fear that those feelings were not reciprocated. Every morning that she woke in his arms only cemented that she was growing too comfortable with him. Frustrated at her predicament, she blew out a calming breath.

"What are you thinking, Lucy?" Trey's husky voice whispered against her hair. His hand stroked along the length of her bare arm and a shiver ran down her spine.

"I'm angry with you," she answered flatly.

Trey shifted and sat up, pulling her into his arms against his chest. "I know you are, and I'm sorry." He kissed the top of her head. "What can I do to make this up to you?"

"Let me go home," she replied knowing that he would not allow that.

"I can't do that." He sighed. "I don't think I want to do that even if I could."

Lucy's gaze flew up to his. "What do you mean by that?"

His mouth turned up in a half smile. "It means I am growing fond of having you with me." He lowered his lips to hers softly kissing and savoring her sweetness briefly. He lifted his head. "Would you like to go for a carriage ride today? Get out of this house for a little while?"

She was surprised at his offer since he had forbidden her from leaving the house without him and even then he had refused to take her off the property. "Do you mean it?"

"I do. We've both been cooped up here. It will do us good to get out. Perhaps a picnic?"

"A Picnic?"

He lifted her to the side and tossed back the covers. "I'll meet you downstairs," he said as he rose from the bed. He leaned down and gave her one final kiss before sauntering out of the room.

Lucy hurried about getting herself bathed and dressed. She thought about his words that he was growing fond of having her with him and wondered if she was reading more into it than she should. She stood in front of the mirror and examined her appearance. She imagined Trey standing behind her, watching her as he wrapped his arms around her, and her heart began to race. She exhaled to regain her composure. There was only one way to find out if Trey was going to explain what he meant. With a final glance at her reflection, she turned and headed downstairs.

Three hours later, Lucy was beginning to wonder if Trey was avoiding returning to the house. They had talked all during their ride and throughout their noon meal, but in truth, nothing was really said. She was beginning to realize that he would never explain himself to her.

"Do you remember the summer that my parents died when we came to visit your family and Saphronia brought one of the new stable puppies with her?" He smiled at the memory and then turned to wait for Lucy's reaction.

A flash of a tiny brown puppy, two giggling girls, and an afternoon spent playing with the pup. She grinned. "I remember," she answered softly. "We had such a good time that day."

He chuckled. "When you think of that puppy, how do you picture him in your mind?"

She cocked her head at his question. "Well, I suppose he was about this big and so soft." She held her hands about a foot apart.

"You know that puppy still lives on one of my estates. He's grown up and rather big now." He lifted his hand about three feet above the ground. "Good dog. But he's not that little puppy any longer." The smile slipped from his handsome face. "It's like Saphronia and yourself. I keep thinking of you two as those two little girls racing after a puppy."

Lucy's face fell, and she felt her heart stop. At that moment, she realized that she had fallen in love with Trey, but he had just destroyed her soul. He thought of her as a child. No matter what had happened, he was telling her that he would always see her as a little girl.

Trey knew he had hurt her and inwardly swore. He turned away and looked straight ahead across the meadow. "I was wrong. The two of you both grew up just like that puppy. And even though I saw it happening, in my mind I kept you both at six years old."

She didn't say a word. If she tried to speak, she knew she would cry.

"I was wrong," he repeated. "These past few weeks with you have made me realize that the two of you have grown up whether I like it or not." He looked back at her and added, "It was never in my mind for you to be a, um, a replacement for anybody. Until that first night here when I saw you in that nightgown, I had never looked at you as anything except a child. Again, I was wrong."

An image of Trey's reaction that night flashed in her mind. He had been caught off guard and had fled the room. "Then why would you provide it for me?"

He snorted and shook his head. "Another error in judgment. I knew you and Saphronia shared gowns from time to time, so I had instructed her seamstress to create a trousseau as a gift for her wedding trip. I wasn't thinking that she would provide a wardrobe that any man would love to see his new bride wearing."

"You left quite quickly that night," she prompted hoping he would add more.

"I did," he answered quickly. "I was shocked to my toes." His own embarrassment caused him to look away. "I had Tim and Daniel sleep outside your room that night to make sure you didn't leave. They were not too pleased with me."

She recalled how tired Tim had been the next morning and couldn't help but grin. "I imagine they were not."

The silence settled over them again until Trey reached over and took her hand. "Lucy, you've been a good sport through all of this, but I swear to you, I never intended to use you in any way that would hurt you. The rest of the world may think what they want of me, but I need you to understand the truth."

Lucy did believe him. She had hoped he had brought her out here to tell her that he wanted her. That he couldn't spend the rest of his life without her. But that hadn't happened. And there was nothing she could do to make him change her mind. And so she gave him the answer he wanted to hear. "I do believe you, Trey," she whispered.

The breath he released was audible to both of them, and they chuckled. Trey's smile widened, and he lifted her hand to his lips. "Thank you for believing me." His gaze held hers for a brief moment and he was overcome by how beautiful she was. "Shall we head back? You will probably want to rest before dinner."

His words startled her. She generally wasn't one for napping unless she had a late night planned. She assumed he was trying to get her out of his hair for the rest of the day. When he rose and offered his hand, she took it without comment. She had read too much into his actions, but now she knew that her feelings were not reciprocated.

"My lady," a voice called softly. Lucy's eyes opened to find Mrs. Grouse standing beside the bed. "I told my lord that the fresh air would tire you out." She smiled warmly.

Lucy stretched and looked beside her, but Trey was not there. "What time is it?" she asked sleepily.

"It must be close to seven," the housekeeper answered. "Now, the boys are bringing you up a nice hot bath, and then I'll be back to help you dress." As if on queue, there was a knock on the door. Mrs. Grouse opened the door to let the footmen and her husband in with buckets of steaming water. After two more trips, Lucy found herself alone.

As she slid down into the hot steamy water, she closed her eyes and sighed, willing the bath to drain away her cares. But even as her body relaxed, her heart was still clenched tight in her chest, knowing that she had fallen in love with somebody who would not love her back in the same way. And it hurt more than she had ever imagined.

She chided herself for trying to tempt him into lowering his guard. Looking back, he must think she was just another hopeless wanton, throwing herself at him in the most unladylike ways. There was just something about being near Trey that made her want to lose herself in him. But he didn't want her that way.

A knock sounded at the door and startled her from her thoughts. She glanced at the door, fearful that it was Trey. When the housekeeper called out, "My lady?" Lucy let out a sigh of relief.

"Come in," she called out and reached for the towel as she stood up in the tub.

Mrs. Grouse entered carrying a peach gown. "Ah, just in time." She laid the gown across the bed with a flourish. "It's been many years, but I have filled in as a lady's maid in a pinch. It will be fun."

"Well, I hardly think I need much assistance here. After all, it's just Chelmsworth." She allowed the older lady to assist her in dressing anyway.

"Nonsense. My lord asked me to assist you, so you must let me or else I could get in trouble with my employer."

An hour later Lucy was dressed with her hair done up in a simple but elegant coiffure. She gave herself one last look in the mirror and was hit with a rush of sadness. She looked as if she were heading out for a London ball, and not a simple dinner. It seemed a cruel waste of her time.

She froze when she reached the top of the stairs. Trey was waiting at the bottom dressed in formal attire. He looked as if he should be attending a ball and not escorting her into dinner in this rustic home. But he was also fidgeting and pacing back and forth. She was wondering what had him so nervous when suddenly he glanced up at the top of the stairs and his eyes met hers.

Trey stared in awe at the beautiful woman standing above him. His heart stopped, and he forgot how to breathe for a moment. He swallowed, twice, trying to regain his tongue. He still could not form words and instead gave her a warm smile.

Lucy's heart melted at the sight of his smile. She took a calming breath and started down the steps, not caring how he felt about her but determined to enjoy their time together while she could.

With each step she took, Trey's heart picked up its pace until he thought for certain she could hear it beating a rapid a tattoo. How had he ever thought she was still a child? She was stunning, and he wanted her in the way he had never wanted another. When she finally reached him, he took her hand and placed a tender kiss on the backs of her fingers. "My God, you are beautiful," he whispered.

A faint blush colored her porcelain cheeks. "Thank you, my lord," she answered shyly as she placed her hand on his arm.

Trey led her to the dining room, and she gasped as she entered the room. It was set in such a strict order that it would have shamed many of London's grand dames' dining rooms. She looked up at the earl in surprise and she grinned. "One must dine before one attends Almack's. Trust me, I've been there before and aside from stale biscuits and tepid lemonade, one learns to never attend without eating."

"Almack's?" she asked in disbelief.

He helped her into her chair and then took a seat close to her instead of at the opposite end as was his normal location. "As it is my fault you have unused vouchers for this evening to the sacred ballroom of Almack's, I have created my own version."

He nodded to Daniel and within minutes they were being served an elaborate dinner. He studied Lucy for her reaction, and she seemed pleased with the fare before them.

"And you planned all of this yourself?"

He chuckled. "Well, Mrs. Grouse had a couple suggestions."

"Just a couple?"

"Actually, once I told her of my idea, she chased me out of her way and told me I would just be underfoot."

Lucy giggled knowing how the housekeeper could be determined. "Well, I must say, you have quite surprised me with a lovely evening."

Trey raised an eyebrow. "Ah, but the evening has just begun. There is much more."

"Do tell," she replied flirtatiously.

"So impatient, Lady Lucinda. You will steal my thunder if I tell you all of my secrets."

Lucy gave him a coy look. "And what could I do to get you to reveal those secrets?"

Trey's hand halted and his wine glass was suspended in midair. There were so many things he wanted her to do. So many things he wanted to do to her. He forced his hand to lift the wine and took a drink, watching her from over the rim. "Come now, we all have secrets. I'm sure you have a few that you would not so easily share."

She blushed again all the way from her forehead to the luscious swell of her breasts and suddenly he desperately wanted to know every secret she held. He yearned to unlock her riddles and mysteries. To teach her more than she could ever imagine.

Lucy felt very warm under his scrutiny. She blinked and looked away, afraid that he could read her thoughts.

Trey reached for her hand. His thumb gently caressed her skin until she faced him again. "Are you ready for the rest?" he asked.

"What is next?"

He chuckled and stood to assist her from her chair. "My dear, once again, you are trying to take away my element of surprise."

She shook her head at his teasing manner and knew this lighthearted, happy Trey was the Trey everybody swooned over. She liked this Trey, and his behavior tonight reassured her that no matter how angry he was with Jack, deep down that kind earl did still exist.

They approached a doorway and Matthew formally opened the doors and then proceeded to announce them. When Lucy cast a quizzical glance the butler's way, he winked at her with a beaming grin on his withered face. Together they entered a beautifully decorated makeshift ballroom. Once again, Lucy gasped.

"Welcome to your ball, Lady Lucinda." He leaned down to whisper in her ear and a shiver of excitement ran through her.

Chapter Nine

Lucy turned her head towards Trey. His face was an inch from her own, and her breath caught in her throat. Her eyes strayed to his lips recalling how his kisses made her feel so alive.

"Will you honor me with a dance, my lady?" His voice was low and husky. He reached for her hand but stopped short from taking it, letting her make the decision. Slowly she slipped her hand in his and they moved to the center of the floor.

"Do we hum or are you going to serenade me?" she teased.

Trey chuckled down at her and then looked away. With a nod, a violin began to play a waltz. Lucy's gaze flew to the corner of the room and noticed Daniel playing a violin. She looked back to Trey wide-eyed. "My goodness, I thought he was a footman."

"A footman who likes to dabble in music," he responded. He placed his hand on her waist and pulled her into his arms. The feeling he experienced when she was in his arms was chilling. She made him feel tranquil, strong, accepted and understood. Instinctively, he pulled her even closer.

Lucy looked up at him. "Is this the acceptable form of dance at Almack's?" Not that she had any objection to being held so closely by Trey.

He grinned down at her. "This isn't Almack's. We can make our own rules." His hand drew her in even more. "Besides, I prefer to have you like this."

Lucy returned the expression. "I find that I prefer to be like this, as well."

Trey chuckled and turned her in a graceful move. "What do you think of your ball, Lady Lucinda?"

"I am quite impressed, my lord," she cooed. "You never cease to amaze me."

They finished the dance in silence, both enjoying the nearness of the other. When the music ended, he sighed and stepped back a half step. She lifted her gaze to his golden eyes, mesmerized by the glow they emitted.

"I can see the stars in your eyes," Trey whispered. When her eyes widened in mortification, fearing he had figured out that she was in love with him until he looked up to the ceiling.

Lucy followed his glance and realized there were a hundred silver paper stars hanging from the ceiling. She grinned at the beauty and the extravagance that had gone into putting this all together. "You had to have planned this for weeks." And then her eyes narrowed. "Was this planned before as well?"

He smirked. "I made a lot of plans, but even I could have never imagined I'd be throwing together a ball. This was spur of the moment. A peace offering for making you miss your first attendance at Almack's." He glanced around the room. "Mrs. Grouse really did outdo herself, didn't she?"

She relaxed and giggled. "She did a marvelous job."

Trey stepped back but left his hand on her waist as he led her towards a small table set up on the side of the room. He picked up a glass of lemonade and handed it to Lucy. "Your tepid lemonade and stale biscuits, my lady. Just like Almack's."

Lucy rolled her eyes. "You better hope Mrs. Grouse doesn't find out you have disparaged her refreshments." She nodded towards Daniel standing patiently in the corner.

Trey laughed out loud. Daniel looked up to find them both staring at them. With a quick jerk of his head, Trey sent the musical footman away. Lucy watched him leave and then turned back to Trey.

"The dancing is over?" she asked.

"For now."

She took a sip of the drink. "What other plans did you make?" Her voice was calm and quiet.

"Excuse me?" he inquired.

She spun to face him. "You planned the wardrobe. What other plans did you make? This home? Do you truly own this home?"

"I do," he answered quickly. "I've been after the owner to sell it to me for years, and he finally relented."

"I can see why you would want it. It is nice to be away from the hustle and bustle of town."

"And do you like it?" he asked hoping for some reason that she would say she did.

She smiled at him. "I think I would like it more if I were here under different circumstances."

Trey was before her in a heartbeat. He took her hands and held them against his chest. "Tell me," he pleaded in a husky voice. "Tell me what circumstances."

She cocked her head in confusion. "Perhaps if I wasn't being used as a pawn for your revenge against my brother for falling in love with your sister."

He kissed her hands softly. "You are not a pawn."

"Then what am I?"

He released her hands and pulled her tightly against his hard body. "You are perfect," he growled as his mouth covered her plump lips. Softly he stroked along her bottom lip, tempting her to open to him. With an intoxicating sigh, she complied and melted against him.

Trey moved to deepen the kiss, probing his tongue inside her sweet welcoming mouth. Heaven, he thought. She was heaven in his arms. He clung to her, exploring her, tasting, tempting himself to take more. One hand slowly moved from her back to the curve of her waist.

Lucy's pulse quickened at the heaviness of his hand at her hip. The fingers of his other hand lightly brushed the exposed span of her neck. She leaned against those digits, and Trey lifted his lips from her own.

He kissed the opposite side of her neck, swirling his tongue against the sensitive spot just below her jawline. His hand moved higher and higher as his lips moved lower along her neck. One long finger traced along the edge of her gown's neckline, feeling the swell of her full breasts beneath his touch.

Trey raised his head and stood up, gazing down at his hands. Desperately wanting to explore more of her, he pushed the top of her gown lower, exposing her mounds to his gaze. A hot breath hissed past his lips. Both hands cupped her breasts, his thumb and forefinger working each peak to a taunt point.

Lucy trembled beneath his scrutiny, afraid that she would do something wrong or that he would not be pleased with her. When he finally met her eyes, she sucked in a breath. She had never seen such burning desire meeting her gaze. Her lips parted to speak, but no words came. Unconsciously, she ran her tongue along her bottom lip.

Trey's eyes followed the movement of that pink tongue and it was his undoing. He wanted her. He needed her. He dipped his head and took her nipple into his searing mouth. She gasped. His tongue flicked and teased the peak, taking her lightly between his teeth, until he suckled her. The small cry that sounded from Lucy rang through his ears and urged him on.

Picking her up in his arms, he carried her to the window seat and sat down with Lucy sideways on his lap. Kissing her neck again, his hand slowly, meticulously, snaked up her leg, from her ankle, along her calf. Higher still, to the soft skin of her thighs. He paused wondering how far he would go.

Lucy was stunned with the sensations he was awakening in her. With each touch, each caress, she was finding a new exhilaration of pleasure. She raised her chin and allow him greater access to her neck, but he removed his lips. Lucy softly moaned her displeasure, but the sound was swallowed by his mouth on hers, kissing her deeply and sparking another round of feelings.

Trey's fingers resumed their tortuous climb until he found the apex of her legs. As he stroked against her most intimate place, he felt her give over to him. He knew he could strip her naked and enjoy each and every delectable inch of her body without any resistance. Her low groan of pleasure as she shifted her legs to allow him easier access gave him pause.

Regretfully, he broke their kiss and looked down at her beautiful face, flush with desire, eyes partially closed. His fingers stilled. Little by little, her eyes opened. He read the confusion in them. "Trey?" she whispered. He could not reply. He had not ever seen a more erotic invitation than the one she was presenting him. "Please," she softly begged.

He closed his eyes. She didn't even understand what she was begging for. He swallowed and took a deep breath. He moved his hand from under her skirts, feeling as if he were leaving a part of his soul by denying her the pleasure he so desperately wanted to give her.

He lifted her to her feet and adjusted the bodice of her gown to cover her flesh. "You should go," he choked out. When she stared at him, he added, "I should go."

Tears filled her eyes. "Why?" she choked out. "What did I do wrong?"

His heart felt as if she had reached inside his chest and squeezed the organ herself. He shook his head and laid a reassuring hand against her cheek. "You were perfect," he answered tenderly. "It's me. I'm the wrong person to take this moment from you. I've possibly done irreparable damage to your reputation. But if there is even a slight chance that my folly is not discovered, I can't destroy you."

"But what about me?" Her voice was desperate for the truth, but Trey could not give her what she wanted. It would seal her fate if he did.

"I must go," he repeated. "I'm so sorry, Lucy. I have made a mess of everything." He turned on his heel and left the room.

The dam burst leaving Lucy knowing what a heartbreak felt like.

Trey stared at the ceiling of the bedroom reliving what had happened downstairs just a short time ago. He knew he had been pushing the boundaries with a stolen kiss here and a tender embrace there. But it was more than just a want. He needed her. He knew that she was not asleep, and he wondered if the same thoughts were disturbing her sleep.

He turned his head slowly to see if she was trying to sleep. Lucy raised her head slightly at his movement. Her eyes heavy with questions and passion. Trey opened his mouth slightly to speak and watched her innocently lick her soft pink lips. The simple action undid him. With a groan, he rolled over and covered her mouth with his own.

Lucy moaned and instantly met his kiss with one just as ardent. Her hands roamed his muscular back caressing each striation with an innocent study. Her tongue sensuously waltzed with his own, a continuation of their earlier sensual dance. A desperate growl boiled forth from Trey's throat, and he shifted his position to hover above her.

"Lucy," he whispered. "This is so wrong, and I know better. Heaven help me, I cannot resist you."

Her hand reached for him. "Please don't resist. I could not bear it," she replied breathlessly.

One hand gently pushed aside the delicate straps of her gown. He pushed the material back to reveal her firm, round breasts. His breath left him for a second as he gazed upon them. He glanced up to her and was met with a curious, nervous stare. He glanced back to her breasts and gave in to the temptation. He lowered his head and captured one of her nipples with his hot mouth.

Lucy sighed at the pleasurable sensation rushing within her body. One hand instinctively came up to rest on the back of his head as if to hold him in place. Just as she thought she would die of pleasure, he lifted his head. A small cry of disappointment crossed her lips until she felt his lips capture her other nipple. The cry turned into a moan of passion.

He pulled her towards him until he could easily raise her gown over her head. He muttered his pleasure and enjoyment at the sight of her fully nude body. Taking a deep breath, he proceeded to explore her offerings.

Trey's hand drifted across her flat stomach admiring her trim figure. Her skin was so soft and smooth. His fingers trailed along her side noting the flare of her hips from her tiny waist. His hand slid down to her thigh and squeezed gently. Lucy's legs moved apart at his light touch.

He raised his head to kiss her again, tenderly, slowly, methodically. As Lucy was consumed by his kisses, she began to realize that his fingers had found her most intimate place and were touching, teasing, and tempting her with promises of more and more. When he slowly inserted one finger within her, she whimpered. Little by little she felt her body respond and then demand something that she didn't quite understand. It was more than a want; it was a desperate need.

Lucy's senses rose higher and higher by his touch until she was soaring and falling at the same time, over and over. She clung to him as she came down from her bliss, her heart racing, her breathing haggard.

Trey had never witnessed something so pure before. He felt honored to have given her such an experience and even more honored to have watched her embrace it. His lips returned to hers, kissing her softly, tenderly, trying to show her how perfect this moment had been for him as well.

Breaking their embrace, he reached for the buttons on his breeches. With each move, he was immediately reminded of what he was about to do. Pushing the pants down his legs and kicking them off, he took a deep breath and returned his attention to Lucy.

Shifting his body between her legs, Trey stared down into her violet eyes wondering if she realized what was happening. The look she gave him was a combination of need, desire, and an innocent pleading that he would be able to give her what she didn't quite know. His head cleared for a fraction of a second willing himself to stop this insanity until she spoke.

"Please," she whispered. "I want this. I want you, Trey."

That was all he needed to hear. Guiding himself to her entry he leaned forward to capture her lips. Pushing forward slowly he met her barrier and paused. His heart was racing, his breathing was ragged. It took all his control to pause and wait for her to relax.

Deepening his kiss, she gave herself over to him completely and he pushed on. A slight cry of surprise emitted from her lips. Trey buried his head in the crook of her neck and bit his hand to keep from reaching his pleasure already. He had never felt such a moment of pleasure this intense. When he finally regained control of his body, he recalled what had just happened. He patiently waited, kissing her tenderly, caressing her face, her neck, allowing her the time she needed to adjust to his invasion. With a long-satisfied sigh, she melted against him and he knew she was ready.

Taking a deep breath, he began to move within her. This time her gasp was one of enjoyment. Her hands came up around his neck and her own hips learned to match his movements. Once again, she felt something building within her even as Trey groaned at her body's reaction. He raised himself up on one arm and returned his fingers between their bodies.

"That's it, love," he encouraged. "Just let it go."

Lucy's head rolled back and forth on the pillow as the need she had been searching for came closer and closer until finally it was reached, and her body exploded into a thousand pieces within. She was just coming down from her high when she heard Trey moan softly at first. Then as his movements increased in pace, his moan turned into a full growl. She watched his face, eyes closed, neck strained, arms shaking until he collapsed on her, resting his weight on his forearms.

His breathing slowed little by little. Lucy's hands caressed his back until he recovered. Taking a final breath, he lifted his head and took in her beautiful face. "How are you? Did I hurt you?" he asked.

"Oh, God no!" she exclaimed. "That was the most beautiful experience I've ever had."

He smiled and kissed her gently. "Me, too," he whispered. He rolled off her onto his back but pulled her into his arms. She rested her head against his chest and sighed. His hands lightly stroked her back while he savored the feel of her.

Trey closed his eyes, but his mind was reeling. He had planned every aspect of his revenge on Jack, followed each step to a tee, and yet somehow everything had been thrown off course. He wasn't supposed to be so attracted to Lucy. He wasn't supposed to be consumed with such desire for her whenever he looked at her. He wasn't supposed to let her into his heart and make him feel this way. And he certainly wasn't supposed to act on those feelings.

Yet here he was. Holding one of the most beautiful, amazing, intelligent women he had ever encounter in his arms in the afterglow of making love. And he didn't want to let her go. Instinctively he squeezed her closer to him. Lucy sighed sweetly. He listened to her breathing and realized she was sleeping. He kissed the top of her head. "What am I going to do with you now?" he whispered.

Several hours later Trey was still awake when Lucy turned in her sleep. She raised her head and noticed Trey watching her, a sweet smile on his face. She returned the gesture sleepily and leaned forward to kiss him.

As their lips touched, Trey responded by pulling her on top of him and drinking in her taste, her lips, her tongue. Lucy moaned innocently at his actions, and it began again. When Trey lifted her to straddle him, she barely seemed to notice until he was sliding into her. He watched her eyes widen first before they slowly closed, and she sighed in pleasure.

Trey lifted her up and down a few times before she picked up the rhythm herself, and then he let her take control. His hands reached up to barely graze her breasts as she rode him. He could tell she was close from her body and her whimpers. It didn't take long before she found her pleasure, and the intensity was so great that he joined with her.

He pulled her down against him, still buried deep within her and kissed her lovingly. She was so innocent, yet so passionate. He couldn't imagine being without her after their three weeks together, but he was also her downfall. He had destroyed her chance at finding happiness on her own.

Suddenly the room felt too small as if the walls were closing in on him. He had to escape. Had to clear his head and think what his next steps were. He moved her to the side of him and started to rise.

"Where are you going?" she asked.

Trey pulled his breeches on and leaned over to kiss her tenderly. "Go back to sleep, love. I'll be back." He tucked the covers around her and watched her close her eyes.

Chapter Ten

Lila Cavanaugh slowed her mount to a walk as she circled the path above the lake. It had been years since she had been here. The lake was rather isolated from Brighton Hall, and it wasn't the same to come here without her husband. She glanced down at the edge of the water and saw Trey sitting on the ground with his head in his hands. She dismounted and handed the reins to a groom. She looked back down at the man who had kidnapped her daughter and sighed heavily before slowly making her way towards him.

"I thought you just might be here," she said. When Trey raised his head to look at her, she stilled at his appearance. He hadn't shaved, his shirt was open at the neck, sleeves rolled up, hair uncombed, eyes bloodshot. "You look like hell."

"That's better than the way I feel," he answered. He hadn't been surprised to see her. In fact, he was shocked it had taken her this long to find him. "She's in the hunting lodge."

Lila lowered herself to sit beside him on the ground. "Ah, and does she know where she is?"

Trey shook his head. The hunting lodge, while near to the property of the estate, was at least five miles from the duke's home, and so isolated in the woods that Lucy had never even known of its existence. It was one of the reasons Trey had brought her here in the first place.

"I remember finding you here another time. Do you remember?" she asked. She watched his face change as his mind recalled the time she was referring. "You were pretty upset then, too."

"My parents had just died, and I was sixteen and responsible for Saphronia," he hissed.

Lila took his hand in both of her hands as she remembered that afternoon. "You were scared, you were sad, and you were so angry." She put her arms around him. "You swore to me that you weren't crying. So stubborn and proud." She held him and rocked him even as she felt his body quake in silent sobs.

He wasn't sure how much time had passed with her motherly arms around him before he found his voice. "I wanted to hate him. I had spent my life trying to protect her from men like him," he mumbled. "Turns out I'm just like him."

The dowager sat up straight and lifted his face to look at her. "Then that is a very good thing." When Trey looked away from her, she continued. "He loves Sophie, heart and soul. If you would only open your eyes you would see that he is completely taken by her, and Sophie with him."

Trey sighed aloud. "I've ruined her," he confessed.

Lila nodded but said nothing. She had known something like this would happen while Trey and her daughter were alone together for too long. Yet she also knew that deep down, Trey was an honorable man.

"That wasn't my plan. I just wanted him to know how it felt to have his world turned upside down."

"And instead you've had your world turned all topsy-turvy instead?"

He nodded and stared off in the direction of the hunting lodge, hidden from his view by the forest. He pictured Lucy still sleeping in the bed they had shared last night. His heart skipped a beat at the image, and he wished he could wake her up and continue where they had left off.

"Trey, my dear." Lila's voice snapped him back to reality. "You were so convinced that Jack ruined your sister without a thought or care, and he couldn't possibly love her. And now you find yourself in the same boat. Swallowing your pride and admitting Jack and Sophie love one another will help you realize your own situation may not be so different."

The dowager stood up with the grace of a queen. "I expect to see you and my daughter at Brighton Hall by noon." With that command, she turned and left him.

Trey found himself staring down at the most beautiful woman he had ever known. Her golden hair lay fanned out on the pillow. Her angelic face gave no hint to the passion that had consumed her just hours before. One slender hand lay upturned beside her head. The sheet had slipped below one breast. His eyes were transfixed on it until he heard her voice.

"Good morning," she purred sweetly.

Trey glanced up at her face and saw his future in her eyes. A shiver ran up his spine. Lucy sat up and reached for him with a questioning look. His hand moved to cradle her cheek. His thumb gently caressed the underside of her jaw. Slowly he bent down and kissed her ever so tenderly.

"Come," he choked out. "We need to dress." He helped her to rise and into her robe. He held her in his arms and rested his chin against the top of her head. Lucy wrapped her arms around his waist and savored the feel of him against her. Finally, he kissed her hair and stepped back. "I'll have hot water sent up for you."

An hour later Trey and Lucy were riding slowly along the road, Lucy was chattering happily trying to bring Trey out of his quiet mood. An odd feeling came over her and she looked forward instead of to her companion. She saw her family's old ancestral home rising before her, and she instantly felt as if she were going to be ill.

Trey knew the second she recognized her location. He brought his mount to a stop and took a deep breath for encouragement before turning to face her. She was wide eyed and open mouthed. "You remember it?" he asked as he dismounted.

"Brighton Hall."

Trey reached up for her and lifted her from the horse. He let her slide down the front of him until she was settled safely on the ground. One hand tucked a stray curl behind her ear. "You are so beautiful and perfect, Lucy. You deserve the very best life has to offer."

Her heartbeat stuttered. What was he trying to say? She loved him, and after last night, she thought he felt the same way. "You are the best life has to offer," she replied nervously.

He pulled her against him and kissed the top of her head. "No, I'm not, Lucy. I can't bring you anything except anger and resentment. You may not see it now, but one day you will thank me."

She gasped and pushed away from him and stumbled backward. Tears in her violet eyes. "You lied. It was all part of your plan. You wanted to destroy Jack by destroying me!" She spun away and cried out in frustration.

"No, I swear to you..." he tried to explain reaching for her.

"And to think, I honestly believed your sweet talk and excuses. I thought you had finally seen the error of your ways. But you had planned this all along." She turned quickly and faced him. "And do you know what the best part of your plan was?" She snorted. "I fell in love with you."

Trey felt as if she had just stabbed him in the chest. He tried to take her hand.

"Don't touch me!" she cried. "Just leave. You've got what you wanted. You humiliated Jack. You stole my innocence, destroyed my reputation, and crushed my heart." She pointed her finger at his chest. "But guess what, Trey? In all of your planning, you failed to realize that at the end of it all, Jack and Sophie are still in love and waiting to become parents. You gained nothing but ruining me!" She turned and began walking toward her family's home.

Trey watched her, knowing that he should follow her, should say something. Reassure her that she was wrong, but he had to get away from her now or he would never let her go. And he was not what she deserved. She would thank him for leaving her someday. He pulled himself up on his horse and left.

"Mother," Lucy cried softly and rushed toward the woman sitting in the parlor.

Lila Cavanaugh quickly put her needlework aside in time to embrace her daughter. The moment mother and daughter touched, Lucy's tears fell uncontrollably. "There, there. It's alright. Everything will be fine now. You'll see," she soothed.

"No, it won't! I'll never forgive him for leaving me!" she wailed.

"He left?" Lila tried to hide her shock. She was so certain that Trey would right his wrong. She had often thought if Trey and her daughter spent any time together, they would recognize what a perfect match they were.

Trey always concerned with living up to his father's stellar reputation and often grew overwrought with nervousness and fears. And Lucy was such a calming influence on those around her. She was drawn to those who needed reassurance. It was a natural gift she had to comfort and encourage others.

Lucy nodded. "He said he wasn't good enough, and I deserved better." The tears started anew.

Lila patted Lucy's back to calm her. "I'm sure he's just fretting over what he has done. He cares for you, I'm certain of it."

"No," she sobbed. "I thought so too, but I was wrong. He only cares about hurting Jack."

"Oh, honey," The dowager said as she rocked her heartbroken child. "I know it hurts, and I know there is nothing I can say that will make it better."

"Your Grace, is everything alright?" Julia asked from the doorway. Kit stood behind her. Upon seeing Lucy, Julia ran to the mother and daughter and fell to her knees. "Oh, Lucy. You're back," she whispered in relief and wrapped her arms around her friend.

James joined Kit in the doorway. "She's safe at least," he whispered.

Kit cast a glance over his shoulder. "Safe, but she appears to be distraught. I just pray that Trey has got a good lead on Jack because Jack will kill him once he gets here."

"Dear, why don't you go upstairs and rest. A good long nap will do wonders for you. You must be exhausted," Lila noted. "Run along with Lady Julia, and I'll be up shortly."

Julia jumped to her feet immediately and helped Lucy stand. "Let's go. A hot bath, too, I should think." She supported her friend with one arm around her waist and led her towards the door where James and Kit parted immediately to allow them to pass.

An hour later with Lucy resting comfortably in bed, Julia found her husband in the library. He glanced up when she entered and immediately stood to welcome her.

He kissed her softly. "How is she?" he asked and wrapped his arms around her.

Julia sank into his embrace. "She's resting now. She doesn't want to talk about what happened right now."

"Damn fool," he sighed. "What in the hell was he thinking?"

"That seems to be the most asked question in all of this," she replied. "Where's James?"

"He rode over to the lodge to see if he could find Trey. Somebody needs to warn him that Jack is on his way."

Lucy stared into nothingness. Five days. Five days since Trey had left her. Five days since she had confessed her feelings to him. Five days since he had broken her heart. Perhaps he was right. He had destroyed her. She would never trust anybody with her heart again. It hurt too much to be wrong.

Isabelle and Anna had arrived three days ago, and each had taken turns with Julia sitting with Lucy and waiting for her to talk. But she couldn't find any words to describe the humiliation and pain she was experiencing.

"Would you like me to read aloud?" Isabelle asked quietly. Lucy's only response was to sigh. Lila Cavanaugh glanced up from her sewing and frowned at her daughter's silence.

"My dear, it's a lovely day outside. Perhaps you would enjoy a walk..."

"Where the hell is he?" a shout came from the hall followed by stomping and more yelling until Jack entered the parlor with Sophie clinging to his arm pleading with him. He stopped short when he saw Lucy. She turned to face him, her cheeks pale.

Jack had never felt so helpless in his life as now when faced with his sister's woebegone expression greeting him. He crossed to her in a rush and took her in his arms. "I swear, I'll make him pay, Lu," he vowed through clenched teeth. "Trey Harrow won't know what his own name is by the time I get done with him."

Suddenly Lucy pushed away from him. "Is that all you foolish men think of?" She shoved him backward, but he didn't budge. "You have no right to say one bad thing about him! I love him more than anything and thanks to you, he left!"

Jack shook his head and looked at his mother. "She's distraught. You should have sent for me instead of letting me find out myself. Now, where is the rat?" His last word was chosen carefully for his wife's sake.

"I'm right here."

Everybody turned and looked at the newcomer standing in the doorway. It was Trey. His gaze went straight to Lucy. When she saw him, she let out a cry of frustration. She rose slowly from her chair. Step by step she moved towards him.

Trey waited, holding his breath, unsure of his reception but desperately longing to have her in his arms. When she reached him, he gave her a weak smile. "Lucy," he whispered.

Lucy stared up at his handsome face, his golden eyes, his haggard appearance. Before anybody knew what was happening, she drew back and punched him in the stomach and then fled the room.

Trey doubled over, caught off guard by her action. He had just started to rise when he was jerked upright. He had just enough sense to dodge Jack's fist before a loud shriek filled the room and both men froze.

Sophie was huddled on the floor in a ball. Jack released Trey and rushed to his wife's side.

"Sophie, what is it?" he pleaded in a panic. "Is it the baby?"

Trey reached her just a second after Jack. "Saphronia," he cried. He took one of her hands. "Talk to me, sweetheart. Tell me what's wrong."

Sophie's eyes opened slightly. "Water and a cool cloth," she whispered weakly.

Jack was on his feet and rushing out of the room in a flash.

Sophie's gaze turned to her brother, and she pinned him with a stern regard. "I'm fine. Go after her. I've bought you time."

Trey stilled as her words registered and then a warm grin crept across his face. "You're truly fine?"

"Yes but stop smiling like a fool or your chance will be over," she hissed. "And Trey?"

"Yes?"

"I'm not very happy with you right now," she scolded and frowned.

That wiped the happiness off his face just in time as Jack returned and pushed him aside to get to his wife. "Here, love," he stated, holding a glass of water to her lips and supporting her back with his other arm. When she had taken a few sips, he handed the glass to Trey. "Let's get you upstairs."

Trey watched as Jack lifted Sophie into his arms. The strained look on his brother in law's face told him that Lucy had been right. Jack was absolutely in love with Saphronia. He also noticed that despite the fear Jack was going through, he was more concerned with seeing to his wife's needs. He waited until Jack had left the room with Sophie safely in his arms, and then he went in search of Lucy.

After spending a good hour hunting for Lucy, he spied her sitting on a bench by the lake. "It was easier to find you when we were at the hunting lodge," Trey called softly.

Lucy didn't turn to face him. "I wanted to be alone," she replied quietly.

Trey moved closer to her and sat down on the bench. "I behaved badly, and for that, I am incredibly sorry, Lucy."

She did not comment and continued to look across the lake.

He ran his fingers through his hair, knowing that he was making a mess of this chance. "I was wrong to leave you. I was afraid, and I ran instead of facing the truth."

She snorted. "I am surprised Jack hasn't killed you yet or is there a duel set for tomorrow morning. Isn't that how you men solve these things?"

"I wasn't afraid of Jack," he replied. "I was afraid of you."

Lucy's head swiveled around. "Me? Why would you be afraid of me?"

Trey took a deep breath. "Do you remember the last time we were on this dock?"

She sighed. "How could I forget? I fell in the lake and you fished me out." She recalled looking at him with wide-eyed hero worship as he carried her inside to the nursery. "I thought you were magnificent."

He chuckled as well. "I know. You even wrote me a note of thanks that same day. Do you recall?"

Lucy blushed at her childish gift. He couldn't fault her. She was a little girl, maybe five or six years old.

"Dear Lord Viscount Harrow," he paused to look at her and she closed her eyes at her childish blunder of his former title. "Thank you for saving my life. You are the bravest, best, and smartest person I know, besides my Father. You can do anything. I am happy you saved me. Sincerely, Lady Lucinda Cavanaugh."

"Well, I was a child. But you're making that up," she corrected.

"Am I?" Trey raised one eyebrow. "Post Script, Please, accept my favorite green ribbon as a thank you. I was wearing it today and it brought me luck. I pray it brings you luck as well."

Her head shot up. The green ribbon. She had forgotten about that. She watched as he reached inside his jacket pocket and removed a folded piece of parchment. Her eyes widened. He opened it and revealed a tattered green ribbon.

"You may not recall what happened that evening, but my parents were killed in that carriage accident. My whole world changed that day."

Lucy couldn't help but reach for him. She placed a hand on his sleeve. "I guess I didn't realize that or else I had forgotten it. I'm sorry. I should have remembered. We were all together for a country house party."

He covered her hand with his own and gave her a warm smile. "It's alright. I wish I could forget it myself."

"I cannot believe you kept that old ribbon."

He held it up by one end and let the other end dangle freely. "It was a sweet gesture, but given the timing and the words, it also gave me the strength to get through those dark days." He let the ribbon fall into his outstretched hand. "My father used to say, 'Trey, you can do anything you put your mind to.' Your note was a reminder of his faith in me."

"I'm happy it brought you comfort," she answered, and she meant it. Even though he had broken her heart and would never love her the way she loved him, she didn't wish him to suffer. It just wasn't in her to will ill on another.

In one fluid movement, Trey was kneeling before her, holding her hands in his. "Lucy, you bring me more than comfort. I told you I was afraid of you, and that's why I had left you. I didn't understand it myself until later that day, but I have fallen in love with you. Those feelings were so foreign to me that I convinced myself leaving you would be better than facing them head-on."

Lucy's heart began to race, and her breath caught in her throat. Surely, she had heard him wrong. She was too afraid to think it might be true and set herself up for an even worse pain.

"You think that I saved you all those years ago, but in truth, it was you who saved me. Over and over for years. And when I was at my very lowest and darkest, you made me realize that I was wrong about Sophie and Jack."

She raised her head to meet his gaze. "You called her Sophie. You've always called her Saphronia."

He chuckled. "I realize now that Saphronia was the little girl who did as she was bid. Sophie is the grown woman who knows what she wants and risks all for those she loves. And she loves her husband as well as her brother. I guess part of me thought I was being replaced, but I see now that there is enough love in her heart for both of us."

"And Jack?" Lucy asked

Trey laughed and shook his head. "Thanks to my sister's stage performance inside, I can clearly see that he loves her. I've never seen Jack so completely terrified and yet so calm. He completely forgot about his death wish for me the second he thought Sophie was ill."

"She's ill?" she gasped

"No," he shook his head. "She was only pretending to occupy Jack so that I could come after you."

Now it was Lucy's turn to giggle. "Ah, Sophie. She's the only one who would dare."

As the silence settled between them, Trey placed one hand along her cheek. "Lucy, I know that what I did to you is unforgivable, but you said that you loved me. I find that I don't know how I will ever be able to go on without you in my life. I love you, and I wish that you would consider becoming my wife. That is if you can ever forgive me."

"You do?" she asked not sure if she dared believe him.

He gave her a boyish grin. "I do." He raised her hand to his lips. "Lucy, you are unlike anybody I have ever met. I enjoy your company, I enjoy your wit, I feel complete when I am with you." Suddenly he dropped her hands and stood up, turning his back to her. "I hurt you, but it was never my intention."

Trey felt as if he had lost his only chance at happiness. He was too ashamed to face her. Had he gotten to know her in the normal manner, he was certain he would feel the same way, and she would have no doubt. But his stubborn pride over Jack and Sophie had destroyed any chance she would ever believe him.

Lucy watched his back and thought about his words. She wanted desperately to believe he had not planned to use her all along, but just when she thought she could believe him, he left her devastated. Hearing his reasoning now, put it all in a different perspective. He wasn't trying to hurt her, he was trying to understand his own feelings.

Trey felt a hand on his shoulder, and he shuddered. This was where she told him that it would never work. That he had killed any chance they might have ever had. He didn't want to hear it and almost walked away. But he owed her the opportunity to give him an ear full. And so he waited.

Chapter Eleven

"Trey," she said softly.

He could not look at her, but he did reach back and cover her hand with one of his own. Lucy felt him tremble.

"Thank you for telling me that. I will be honest with you as well. I was truly hurt to think that you could leave me after what had happened, after what I thought was a special night. And I wanted to die over the pain I felt when I thought that it meant nothing at all to you."

She moved around to face him. He took a deep breath and opened his eyes, prepared to see a look of scorn and rejection staring back at him. Instead, he was met with her sweet, kind, understanding gaze that bore right into his soul and assured him everything would be fine.

"Trey Harrow, I love you, and I am very happy that you came back." She smiled warmly at him.

"Do you mean it?" he asked nervously.

Lucy had barely nodded when he pulled her into a tight embrace and pressed his lips to hers. He kissed her tenderly and then raised his head. "And will you be my countess?" She grinned and bobbed her head quickly. He returned the grin for a moment before pulling her to him again.

This kiss was anything but chaste and tender. He stroked her soft lips until they parted and then delved inside to explore her sweet offering. Lucy clung to him, fearing that if she let go this would all be a dream. He made her lose her head when he kissed her this way, and especially now that she understood the other ways he could make her feel. A small moan sounded from her throat, and Trey reluctantly lifted his head.

He sighed. "Lucy," his voice was barely a whisper. "We better stop before I push Jack over the limit."

She blinked in confusion. "I thought he was with Sophie."

"Was," he clipped and nodded over her shoulder.

Lucy turned to find Jack standing no more than ten paces away, arms crossed, legs spread shoulder width, and a furious expression on his face. She turned back to Trey and giggled. "He does look a bit angry."

Trey rolled his eyes. "I know that feeling well." He stepped back from her. "I suppose you should allow us some time to sort this out."

"Please don't behave badly. He is my brother after all, and he only feels overly protective of me," she reminded him.

He raised an eyebrow. "I believe that brotherly protection is what started all of this."

She smiled warmly at him before walking towards her brother. Jack's stance did not change but his face softened.

"Are you alright?" he asked, the concern evident in his question.

"I am better than that, Jack. I am in love, and I am going to marry Trey, and if you so much as lay a finger on him, I will not forgive you anytime soon."

Jack frowned. "My wife has made a similar promise," he muttered. His face softened before he added, "Is this what you truly want?"

Lucy nodded. "More than anything."

He shook his head before hugging her. "Then run along inside while we hash this out."

"Don't you dare touch him," she scolded as she walked away.

"How is my sister?" Trey called as Jack approached him.

Jack glared at him. "You're an ass. She's already confessed her deceit."

Trey smirked and then sat down. Jack joined him on the bench, and the two men sat in silence for several moments. "I love her," Trey said breaking the stillness.

"So you say," Jack replied. "But you also forget that I know who you are." His words were an echo of Trey's very same words to him when Jack had tried to convince Trey that he loved Sophie.

"I deserve that," he admitted. "I didn't plan it this way."

Jack wanted to laugh at the irony of their situation. He doubted that he would ever believe Trey, just as Trey would probably never fully believe him. "Funny how that happens."

"I'll be good to her. She'll never want for love or happiness."

"And what of your collection of actresses and widows?"

Trey raised his chin to calm his anger. "I imagine the same thing that will happen to your vast collection of females."

"I am head over heels in love with my wife and have no reason to let my eyes wander."

Trey tried to cover a snort with a forced cough. Jack shot him an annoyed glare.

Trey sighed. "Are we just going to trade barbs or are we going to get down to the current situation?"

"Do you love my sister?" Jack snapped.

"I do," Trey answered quickly.

Jack stood up and turned away. "My wife has forbidden me from touching you for your misdeed, and I've agreed." He paused. "As long as my sister remains happy. But should you ever hurt her or break her heart or violate her trust, I will take great pleasure in destroying you."

"I understand," Trey replied. "As you are also under the same promise with my sister."

"I cannot believe they did not come to blows," Isabelle stated as she shook out Lucy's gown. The bride's bedroom was crowded with all five girls and the bride's mother as they prepared to help Lucy dress for her wedding.

Sophie laughed. "I told Jack that if he so much as touched my brother, he would be sleeping in a separate room until this child was old enough to talk."

Julia chuckled. "And he believed you?"

She blushed. "He seems to want to give me everything my heart desires."

Anna laughed. "You've got him wrapped around your little finger, you mean."

Lila Cavanaugh smiled knowing that her son adored his wife so much. For years she had feared he would never settle down, but now that he had married, she was pleased to know he was captivated by his lovely bride.

Sophie reached for the dress Isabelle was holding. It was a stunning pink, the perfect color for Lucy. "I've never seen this gown before," she noted.

Lucy smiled shyly and glanced at her mother quickly before looking at the gown. "It was my mother's wedding gown," she said quietly. When Lila had shown it to her, the dowager told her she had brought it along knowing Trey would fall in love and end up marrying Lucy.

"You will look lovely in it," Anna stated. "I imagine Chelmsworth won't be able to take his eyes off you."

"Or his hands," Julia giggled and when Lucy blushed, the other girls' laughter joined in.

Lila picked up on the signals. She was once a young lady herself and remembered there were certain things one just didn't tell their mother. "I think I will go check on the preparations downstairs. You ladies seem to have this in hand."

The second the door closed, Sophie spun towards Lucy. "Let's have it. I want all the details, starting with what happened the night he took you."

The next forty-five minutes was spent drawing the details of her ordeal out of Lucy. The other girls oohed at the romantic gestures and gasped at the frustrating actions. When she was finished, Lucy reflected back on her adventure with Trey and felt it must be fate that brought them together. She doubted that had they both remained in London they would have fallen in love.

Trey's first thought upon waking was the delightful feminine form curled against him. His eyes opened slowly and looked at his wife. His wife! A month ago, he would have laughed at anybody who had told him he would marry Lucinda Cavanaugh, but now he couldn't imagine how he had could survive without her. Leaning up on one elbow, he gazed down on her sleeping form.

Lucy sighed at the movement beside her. Her eyes fluttered open, and she recognized her surroundings as the bedroom in the hunting lodge she and Trey had shared.

"Good morning, Countess," Trey said softly. "Did you sleep well?"

She smiled at him as he hovered over her. "I don't recall you letting me sleep all that much."

He raised his eyebrows quickly in a teasing manner. "Perhaps we should just spend the rest of the day in bed."

She laughed. "And what would we do if we spent all day in bed?"

"My only purpose in life is to keep you happy and pleased," he stated and rolled his eyes.

Lucy cocked her head. "Do I detect sarcasm?"

"For you dear, never." When she continued to stare at him, he sighed. "Your dear brother informed me that I am to keep you happy or else."

She frowned. "Are the two of you going to behave like this for the rest of our lives?"

"That's up to him," he chuckled. "I would prefer to do as he says and please you." He leaned down and kissed her softly.

"I should hope so, for I plan to spoil my niece or nephew, and I want our children to grow up knowing their uncle as well."

"Our children?" he whispered.

"I want a large family," she answered. "I want my children to have siblings close to their age, so they can also be friends."

"Well, in that case," he grinned and moved his body to cover her. "We had better get started."

Lucy giggled. "Are you certain?"

"I've never been more certain in my life," he answered and then he proceeded to show her just how certain he was.

The Duke's Misgivings

James, the Duke of Kettering, and Lady Isabelle Albany have become close friends over the years after watching their friends pair up one by one and marry. But Isabelle had no desire to ever marry, convinced that a man would only be after her dowry, and James had not found the one who takes his breath away and leaves him begging for more. As a result, the two have become a protection for one another to avoid those they find undesirable.

When Isabelle is set up by an unsavory fortune hunter, hell bent on compromising her to get his hands on her much-needed dowry, James happens to be in the right place at the right time and steps in, letting society believe that he has compromised Isabelle and offering to marry her.

Isabelle finds herself subjected to public ridicule and scorn while James is met with sympathy and pity at this turn of events. James finds himself torn between accepting his fate and revealing to Isabelle the truth of his darkest secret, knowing that the truth would send her running away forever.

Isabelle has her own secrets and fears telling James the truth will make him despise her. Can this mismatched couple accept the future fate has cast them in or will their secrets leave them each alone forever?

Enjoy These Other Books

By Linda Kaye

Coming Home

If you want to catch up with The Trouble With Brothers Series, be sure to read these:

The Viscount's Mishap

The Duke's Mistake

About The Author

Allow me to introduce myself. I am Linda Kaye, a writer of historical romance novels and novellas.

As for my characters, I want them to be realistic. We all have flaws, and characters in a novel should as well. I want characters that come alive on my pages and stand out in your memory, even if they are not the type of person you would want to have as a friend!

Aside from writing I work full time and I am a mother of a son and a miniature dachshund. I enjoy reading (obviously!), genealogy, counted cross stitch, and watching football and baseball.

Some of my favorite authors and books are Harper Lee's "To Kill a Mockingbird", Laura Ingalls Wilder's "Little House Series", Johanna Lindsey, Kat Martin, and Eugenia Price

www.lindakayebooks.com

Made in the USA
Lexington, KY
07 January 2019